I0517479

Gideon's Goս

Gideon's God

Dick Sullivan

Coracle Books

By the same author:

Prose
Old ships
Navvyman
Undertones: Mild Mysticism in an Age of Umber
Counter-Cosmos: the Mind of the Mystic

Poetry
Capperbar
Melanie
The Moon at Midnight
Morning on the Mountain

ISBN 978 0 906280 14 0

for Mary

Contents

CHAPTER I

Midsummer's Day 2004

Porlock paid off the taxi on the harbour. It was a hot summer's day with a scent of sea, and gulls calling. The wooded hills and up-river creeks were covered from crest to shoreline in summer green trees. He had four hundred thousand pounds and a pension and had cut himself off from his own past in order to begin again.

The little fishing port was crowded with tourists. It had turned noon and all the quay-side tables, each with a striped umbrella, were full. At one sat a solitary woman in a slightly shabby summer frock. Porlock picked up his old fashioned canvas grip and rucksack and strolled over. "Excuse me," he said politely, "is this free?" He pointed at an empty chair. She smiled and pushed her cup to one side as though to make room for him.

"Just starting your holiday?" she asked.

"No," said Porlock. "I'm looking for something called *Gideon's God*. Do you know it?"

"Goodness, no," she said. "What is it? A Buddha?"

"Why do you say that?"

"It sounds like a little round statue."

"Could be a statuette," he conceded, "but probably not a Buddha."

Porlock turned to the menu as the waitress (waiter? server? How the old order changeth, he thought) came over in tight blue jeans and a tighter T-shirt. Before she could speak, or Porlock could order, his new companion stepped in: "This gentleman's looking for .... whose God, did you say?"

"Gideon's. *Gideon's God*."

"No, I'm so sorry, my dear," said the waitress, looking puzzled. "I've never heard of it. What is it, exactly?"

"Probably a work of art of some description or other."

"Oh, well, in that case, my lover, then you'd best ask Janice.

She keeps the art shop down off Fore Street." She told Porlock how to get there and then said: "Is there anything I can get you to eat, sir?"

"A bacon baguette, I think, and a cup of tea." The waitress/waiter/server left with his order but his new friend stayed put with her handbag on her knees. Her cup was empty, ringed by a brown froth of milk and coffee. The tide was making. "Pity the summer can't last forever," she said, making conversation. Porlock agreed. He glanced at her from time to time: she looked worn and tired. The young woman in the tight T-shirt brought his order. "The food here's very tasty," his new companion began again after a long silence. "Particularly the pastries. It's part of the restaurant, you know."

"Oh, yes."

"It's called Anson's. I don't know why."

"Probably after the admiral."

"The admiral?"

"He circumnavigated the globe," Porlock added, "and made a fortune when he captured the Manila Galleon from the Spanish. A treasure ship. Very romantic, if bloody. In the 18th century sometime."

"They do say it's like a wooden ship inside."

"You've never been in?"

"Well, it is a bit expensive." Lines of yachts were moored in the stream. A big orange and blue RNLI lifeboat lay ready at her mooring.

"Is your wife joining you?" the woman asked.

"I'm unmarried," replied Porlock, caught off-guard. He was more interested in the river and the hills beyond than in talking to anybody, least of all a complete stranger. To their right, just in sight, a very yellow sandy beach gleamed in the sunshine. How did you reach it? he wondered since it was encased in a great dense loop of trees. He finished his meal and reached for his bags.

"Oh," the lady said, "are you going?"

"Well, I have finished," he said, reasonably. "It's been nice meeting you," he added out of politeness.

" It's a small place. Perhaps we'll meet again."

"You never know," Porlock agreed.

"I hope you find your God."

"Thank you. It'll be a start."

He settled the bill and set off along Fore Street which, following the line of the river as it did, was the key to the town. It was one-car wide and lined with painted two-storey houses, cafés and shops – primrose yellow, beige and blue were the favourite colours. Narrow alleys gave glimpses of the sun-blued river and led down to landing stages, small wharfs, or just steps dipping down into the briny water. Janice's shop – called *Art for All* (it said so on a sign shaped like a painter's palette and mahl stick) – was down one of them, next door to a 17th century fishermen's pub. To get to it, you had to climb an outside flight of wooden stairs, covered in ivy.

It was, he found, a gallery cum shop: paintings by local artists hung on the walls but you could also buy books, reproductions, prints, posters, post cards, colouring books, paints, chalks, crayons, brushes, paper, canvases, frames and easels. A man in sandals and a paint stained smock studied a tube of Winsor and Newton cobalt green acrylic. "Janice," he called out in a loud voice. "Shop. Customers." Janice was nice looking, not handsome, in her late thirties, with mouse coloured hair and glasses of a kind no longer fashionable. "Can I help?" She smiled in a friendly way.

"Well, it's a bit of a long shot but have you ever heard of something called *Gideon's God*?"

"The painting, you mean?"

For a moment Porlock was speechless – shocked, even, and not a little taken aback. "Wow," he said at last. "A bit of a short shot after all. It isn't in any reference book. Neither Google nor Yahoo know anything about it. But you do?"

Janice laughed. "To be honest, I hadn't heard of it myself until a few weeks ago."

"And it is a *painting*, is it? You've seen it?"

"Well, yes, it is a painting but no I haven't seen it?"

"You know where it is?"

"Well, yes," she answered. "As the crow flies, it's about a mile from here. Or by boat. A bit more by road."

"So much for my long quest," said Porlock, ruefully.

"It belongs to Margot Montague in the old Rumblestone Inn," Janice went on.

"The Rumblestone?"

"Yes, a hotel. We always call it an inn, for some reason. It's on an island. Or at least it's an island at high tide. A tidal island I think they call them. They had a big painters' colony all around here at one time. Gideon was one of them."

"So Gideon was a man, was he? Not the character in the Bible?"

"Bible? Oh, no. No, certainly not. I don't know anything else about him but I suppose he must have been part of the artists' colony here in the 1920s, or '30s, I'm not sure which. Margot may have actually known him. Her mother certainly would have. It was a real painters' inn in those days."

"Smugglers' before that," chipped in the painter, swapping cobalt green for Winsor blue.

"Smuggling, too," Janice agreed. "The stone's riddled with caves."

"Pilchards before that," the painter persisted. "A monastery before that. And long before that it was probably a trading post where Phoenicians came to trade for tin with the locals."

"Well, perhaps," said Janice, doubtfully. "Some people like to thinks it's the old Ictis."

"All very Boys' Own," the painter went on relentlessly. "Especially the legend of Old Jem Patch."

"Those stories are true, though, aren't they, Paul?"

"Is it on display, do you know, the painting?" Porlock broke in. "Would Mrs Montague let me see it."

"Margot never married," Janice explained. "And, no, it's not on display at the moment. But it might be on Saturday. She's opening the old ball room up as an art gallery. I'm moving part of my stock in as well. Would you like a flier?"

"Oh, yes, please," Porlock replied diplomatically. "Perhaps I could stay there?"

"You can phone from here, if you like. The mobile signal's a bit weak over there."

Porlock booked a room over Janice's phone, quoting his Visa Card number. Out of politeness, he then looked round the gallery. On the whole the paintings weren't too good. Mostly they were figurative, though some of the seascapes were close to abstract. The flowers were best, along with some still lifes after the manner of Cézanne: subdued lemons and red tulips with a glazed jug and coffee pot – that kind of thing. Mushrooms and garlic were also nicely done. One picture of a sailing dinghy heeling over in a stiff breeze on the river outside the gallery was quite accomplished. But in another a man, lost in a wood, stood with bent arms which if, unfolded, would have scraped the ground: he could, in fact, have washed his feet while standing bolt upright. On the whole, the landscapes also were pretty poor: none could open up that other world – which Porlock sometimes called The Great Elsewhere – and that was the way he judged all art.

Within half an hour, he was in his second taxi of the day. "On holiday?" the driver asked him.

"No, not really," replied Porlock. "I'm starting all over again, for one last time." (Well, for the second time, he corrected himself silently.)

"Enjoy it while you can, my 'andsome. We don't last long, do we?"

"No," Porlock agreed. And then more wholeheartedly: "No, you're right there."

The sun was already on its way down behind them as they drove east along the high ground under the woods on the hills above the sea. Ten minutes later they opened up Rumblestone Bay and the jumble of an inn on a few acres of the green parabola of an island. The sea was a deep blue, sparkling in the sun.

"Wow," said Porlock boyishly, "look at that, will you?"

"Pretty sight, ain't it?" said the driver.

"Incredible. Stunning, in fact."

"Never fails."

"I imagine not."

"Tide's well on the flood," the driver went on. "The island's already almost cut off by the sea. At low tide, you can then walk to the island across the sand."

"Is the whole island left high and dry?"

"No, no, only this side. The water's very deep on the other. Never dries out, does that side. Treacherous, too."

"Is there a boat across?"

"Nothing so common," the driver said. "Old Jake Jewell takes you over on his tractor-ferry. You can see it over by the island, below the white building. See?"

"It's weird."

"It is that," said the driver. "Nothing else like it, not anywhere in the world," he added with a touch of local pride.

The taxi turned down the hill. They drove down the combe, first between hedges and fields and then through a new village of bungalows, like a suburb of the old hamlet which still stood at the river mouth. At the bottom of the hill, the driver slowed right down by a beach shop and a café next to two car parks: a big public one and a smaller, gated, one for hotel guests only. To the east, a long sandy beach was fairly crowded with holiday-makers and the bay with wind-surfers. "There's a phone on a post at the end of the jetty," the driver told him. "Just pick it up if you want old Jake to come for you. Mind you, he's a miserable old bugger at the best of times and making a special trip is never going to be one of *them*. But at this time of year's there's regular crossings. A crowd'll be along soon, you see if they're not. The pub on the other side's a big draw for tourists. Locals too in the winter."

"I'll wait." Porlock paid the driver and lifted his grip and rucksack off the back seat. "I'm in no hurry." The wooden jetty was scented with tar and creosote in the hot afternoon sun. The sea lapped. He waited for the ferryman

CHAPTER 2

Flashback: March 2004

As she said, Janice Maddox had known about *Gideon's God* for only a few weeks, only from the time, in fact, when she and Margot had begun seriously organising the new art gallery in the inn. Gideon's name was in the hand-written inventory of paintings stored in the inn's cellar. Janice read through it one morning in March at the breakfast bar in her kitchen. "Gideon Comely," she'd said to her daughter. "Isn't this a lovely name, Fliss? Gideon Comely," she'd repeated. "What a lovely name for a painter."

"Yes, but are his paintings lovely too?" Felicity, her down to earth daughter, had asked.

"I don't know."

"Why don't you?"

"Because I've never seen any. Margot only has the one, and that's still stored away in the cellar. It has a lovely title, though – *Gideon's God*?"

"Gordon Bennet," her husband, Freddie, snorted. "Not more arty-farty rubbish? I ask you!"

"Freddie, why must you always try to spoil things for your daughter?"

"I don't. I speak the truth, that's all. You're the one trying to brainwash her. Be fair, Janice. What good is all this art?" he asked, reasonably. "Just tell me that, eh? And just how many painters make real money?"

"Dad says you can't eat paintings," Fliss said by way of appeasement.

Janice ignored her. "You're not exactly a multi-millionaire yourself are you?" she snapped at her husband. (She saw their daughter flinch. 'Why,' she asked herself yet again, 'do I let him goad me like this?')

Freddie stood up and smirked. "I will be," he'd said. "I will be. Time will tell." He'd patted his daughter on the head and left the kitchen, and then the house.

"Money is important, isn't it, Mum?" Felicity said, again as a kind of arbitration between the two.

"Enough is, Felicity. All you need is enough. After that other things become much more important. Like going to school and learning things," she'd added.

"That costs money, too, Dad says."

"I know, Fliss, I know. I did say enough is all you need. And, any way, you could eat paintings if you put them on pastries. Can you imagine *The Haywain* on one of those big square flat cakes?"

"Or that horrible bald old man with squiggly lines …"

"Picasso, you mean?"

"Yes, him," said Fliss. "On puff pastries. You wouldn't notice the lines are all squiggly with flaky pastry."

"No, or what about those little miniature portraits on old English muffins?" Janice said.

"The butter would spoil them." Fliss thought about that. "And toasting them would change the colour."

"Burnt umber?"

"Burnt *black*!" Fliss shouted.

"Burnt black? You'd never get tired of them, though, would you? Everybody gets hungry every day. You'd want pastry-paintings for breakfast, lunch and supper".

"Why don't we tell Daddy? He could sell them at tea-time."

By now Freddie Maddox had reached his office in Anson's, the restaurant he both leased and ran. He sat for a moment behind his big desk overlooking the harbour. Winter was just about over over, summer not yet begun. The rain had lifted and sunlight sparkled on the water. All the same, he'd noticed that the RNLI lifeboat had left her moorings. Some stupid bugger was in trouble, he grumbled.

He picked up the phone. "Gabriel?" he said when it was answered. "Freddie Maddox here."

"Hello, Freddie, my old son. How are things by the seaside?"

"Fine, Gabe, fine. At the moment, that is. I'll soon be thinking of getting ready for the new season. It's like opening the sluices to let the cash flow in again. Speaking of which, there's a reason for this call. The painter that Gino kept burbling on about the last time we met? Comb-lee-o or something. It couldn't be Comely would it?"

"Not only could be, Freddie, but is."

"I think I may have located one."

"Where?"

"Down here."

"Well, that figures. A whole slew of painters got down there at one time. How much for it, do you think?"

"I doubt very much it's for sale."

"On what wall is it hanging on then?"

Freddie hesitated. "It's not on any wall at the moment. The wife's involved with the old biddy who owns the inn on the rock down here. You know it, of course?"

"I do. The old boiler won't buy my wine."

"Well, they're opening an art gallery, of all the useless things to do."

"The painting's in this gallery?"

"No, it's not open yet. The picture's still in storage down in the cellar somewhere."

"Could you find it down there?"

"What have you in mind, Gabriel? A spot of larceny?"

"Something like that. I don't think you know old Reggie Bradshaw?"

"No."

"No. Well, he's a solicitor. *Was* a solicitor – he must be eighty if he's a day. He was always a bit on the bent side but never struck off or unfrocked or whatever happens to them when they take a wrong turning. Old and a bit doddery but still got all his marbles *and* he can fix up a foolproof provenance for us."

"And what's that when it's at home?"

"A history of who's owned a painting since it was first made. It makes it all legit and above board."

"I'm all in favour of that. Could we really get away with it?"

"I don't see why not. Comely's not well known. In fact, he's almost completely unknown. I've only ever met one person who's remotely interested in him at all."

"Would it swing the deal, in that case, do you know?"

"Good chance, Freddie. Well worth a try, I'd say.

Very well worth it. After all, what have we got to lose? A painting nobody else wants and nobody else will miss. When's the gallery opening?"

"Second week in June."

"Right, and what is it now? Late March. Well, that gives us enough time at least. We can't very well lift it from the gallery walls. Can you find a good local tea leaf?"

"Yes, I know just the man"

"You *do* know him? Personally, I mean?"

"Yes, I've used him once before. Should be a doddle this one. There's no security over there at all."

"Sounds good, Freddie. All the same, you'd better get your skates on. Meanwhile, I'll rope in old Bradshaw and set him to work. What's the painting called, by the way?"

"*Gideon's God.*"

"Good God, is it? Creepy. Does it mean Gideon is God? Still, better than thinking you're Napoleon, I suppose. At least it shows ambition. And the date?"

"You need to know that?"

"Of course. Not the real date, if you can't get one, but close enough to sound authentic."

"Leave it to me, Gabe. I'll find it and let you know."

"Don't ask the missus, though."

"Give me some credit, Gabriel, for God's sake. Janice has an inventory. All I need is a quick butcher's and we're away."

"All right, Freddie. You're happy to act down your end?"

"Leave it with me. Fingers won't point our way if it all goes pear shaped. I'll see to that."

"I'll phone Gino, as well, to keep him in the frame. Your Italian's not up to it yet."

"His English neither."

"True, Freddie. If he copies you he'll end up speaking like TV villain."

"Well, I'll end up talking like the Mafia if I copy him."

"He's a good kid. He's clean. Just what we need. Okay, old boy. I'll be down in a week or so and we can meet up again. Let me know the date as soon as you like."

"By tonight at the latest."

"Fine. See you, then, Fred."

Freddie put down the phone and looked out of the window. It was still too cold for out-door tables. No grockles to sit there either. Hot summer, when Porlock would sit by the harbour eating a bacon baguette, was some weeks away. At that moment, in fact, Porlock was in the big city on the verge of making up his mind about his future.

That evening Freddie phoned Gabriel again. "The date's 1923," he'd said. "June, 1923. Just as well I checked it out – the date is also part of the title."

"Part of the title? In what way?"

"The full title is *Gideon's God 1923*, without a comma."

"Well done, Freddie. Probably not a jailhouse clanger that one, but it's always best not to drop any clangers at all. And the signature?"

"G dot Comely."

"Is that how he usually signed?"

"Don't know, Gabe. No way of finding out, either. Only the old bat might know."

"Yes, and we can't ask her. Never mind, it's what it's says on the canvas that matters. And we can check that out as soon as we lay hands on it. Luck's with us, Freddie, old son. We're going to pull this one off."

"I hope so, Gabriel. I really do."

"When you hang up, Freddie, have a drink – to our first ten million, pounds that is, not euros."

CHAPTER 3

June 2004

The sea tractor ferry was like a iron tray mounted on struts and stays and those big back wheels of farm tractors. Passage was free to hotel guests, two pounds for punters heading for the old pub. Standing room only: even the driver stood on his own little platform – what looked like folding benches were, in fact, life rafts. The whole contraption rusted in the salt air and sea spray: even the steering wheel, which was handled at each quick crossing, was red with it, as were the rails. A translucent roof arched over all and a very noisy diesel engine drove the ferry through the sea. When the tide was fairly high, the wheels ran completely submerged. Like a boat, the ferry left a wake behind her: not churned up water, however, but sand.

About half mile separated island from mainland. A quarter of a mile across, the island's architecture and lay-out became clear. The 14th century pub, just above the high water mark, was the oldest building by far – even counting the ruined hut on the crest of the hill, maybe three hundred feet above the sea. Six centuries, in fact, separated the pub from the main building which was a little higher up the hill. White balconies with turquoise green window frames ran the full length of the hotel – wrapped themselves completely around it. The all-concrete hotel was topped with a kind of belvedere, out of bounds to guests. It had been begun in the late 1920s but, aesthetically, it was pure 1930s Art Deco. The old wooden Victorian inn stood between the concrete one and the sea. It was clapboard-built, now blistered and peeling, and seemingly built by a carpenter and a bricklayer's mate without a blueprint or plan, full of nooks and odd crannies with half floors and snugs. Staff lived there.

The inn itself was gated, cut off from the trippers who drank in the old 14th century pub. Three steps, a porch, and the reception desk was just inside to the left, discreetly recessed. The receptionist on duty was a jolly-looking middle aged woman with a local accent. Porlock checked in and asked about *Gideon's God*. "A painting is it?" the receptionist said. "You'd best speak to Margot, my darling. Come along this way, my handsome. She's in …. do you know, I don't know what to call it – ballroom or art gallery. It hasn't been used for years and years. My dear life, it was such a dust heap when we opened it up again. And droppings. *Drop*pings."

"Droppings?"

"Mice. Horrid things." She stopped just outside a set of double doors. "I shouldn't have told you that, I expect?"

"I keep secrets," Porlock confided. He thought she was about to wink, but stopped herself and pressed down on the gilt handles, then stepped aside to let Porlock go first. "Margot," she called to a large elderly lady at the bottom of the long room. "Gentleman here is staying with us and wants to know about a painting. Mr Porlock," she added by way of introduction. "I'll leave you to it then." And she did.

Margot hobbled towards him leaning on a stick. Porlock hurried over to save her the effort. They shook hands. "Janice Maddox rang to tell me about you," Margot explained. "I am going to hang the picture in here but it's in storage at the moment. Can you wait until tomorrow or the day after? Is that all right?"

"Of course," said Porlock. "You've hung one or two already, I see. Or is it hanged?"

"Hung on a gallows. Hanged in a gallery." Margot smiled. "Here we keep our country ways and aren't so fussy. Let me show what we've hung or hanged already."

She led him back down the long room and stopped in front of a midnight view of the local bay in midnight blue and mauve with exploding stars and a midnight sea streaked with yellow lamplight from the shore. It felt cold and wrong (but the right kind of wrong) like the view from a ship taking you on an unwanted voyage to an unwanted shore. "The view from a troopship, I think," said a voice behind them.

"That's uncanny," said Porlock. "You read my thoughts."

"Either that or that's what the painting's all about. To those with the right experience."

"The troopship's not bound for old Blighty's shore, then."

"Nor leaving Bombay."

"This is JJ," Margot interrupted. JJ was an elderly man with a tobacco wheeze and a nicotine tinged beard. "I'm a kind of painter," JJ added as though explained all there was to know about him.

"And this is Mr Porlock."

"Not *the* man from Porlock?"

"No, sir. Porlock itself. The real thing."

"You've heard the joke before?"

"A time or two. Not for a few years now though. Xanadu's all but forgotten. It's all in the past."

"We are the past," said JJ. "How does it go? 'Where Alph the sacred river ran through caverns measureless to man down to a sunless sea.'"

"Hateful place," Margot chipped in. "I can't imagine sea without sun, or sun without sea. I've lived a long life surrounded by both. This is one to cheer the old folk up," she went on without pausing. She stopped in front of a painting of untidy flowers in a creamy kind of white on a dark, almost black, olive green background. "The artist was ninety when he painted this. He painted it right here in the inn as well, in the late 1920s."

"You don't remember him, surely?" Porlock asked in astonishment.

"Just. Enormous white whiskers like a baby's bib, and something of the baby's bottom about his face which many very old men used to have in those days, I seem to remember. Mind you, I was a very little girl at the time."

The receptionist reappeared and called Margot away. JJ went with her. "Do look around, Mr Porlock," Margot invited him. "Make yourself at home."

He did. The ballroom/gallery was, in Porlock's words, incredibly beautiful. Windows down one side overlooked a terrace and the terrace overlooked the sea as far as the most distant headland. In between lay rocks, in the shape of a hawk in flight, which were uncovered by each ebb tide.

One end was a concrete replica of the stern cabin of an 18th century man o' war. The stern windows looked out, distantly, to the sea and, in the foreground, the top of a cliff and the slope up to the summit of the island. A sailing ship's wheel was set up in front of the window while, immediately outside, was a pintle and rudder of rusted iron and rotten timber. This was to be Janice's abode for the sale of new paintings and stone sculptures. Buyers could also place orders here for reproductions of the older works hung on the wall. (People could also buy via a new website which had just been set up.) Streaming evening sunshine created windows of shade and light on the floor/deck.

For all the Sailing Navy theme, it was very much an inter-War years room. Young ladies in cloche hats and tube-like frocks must once have sat there on gilded chairs waiting for young men in white flannels and bright blazers up to ask them to dance. They called it the painter's inn, and so it was, but a parallel cosmos catering for gentility also existed alongside it. For the genteel, a quintet in evening gowns played dance tunes among the potted palms in the stern cabin. Were there paintings of dancers and players from that time? Would they be hung?

His room was one of the few without a view, being one of five at the end of a stubby corridor, an afterthought tacked on in the old inn's heyday. It was next to a tall outcrop of stone which you could touch through the opened the window.

Oddly (or so he thought) the bath was next to the bed and not in a separate room (though the lavatory was – a space too tight for a broad shouldered man, which Porlock most definitely wasn't). The bath was like nothing he'd ever seen: the back rose in a graceful curve so that you lie upright with your bead resting on it rim. Its outside was black with silver feet. The pipes were not part of it but came up out of the floor. He had the choice of a bath or a shower – but no shower curtains. When lying in the tub he had a view of the lichened stone outside the window. While shaving in the morning, he also discovered, he had the same view in the oval 1930s mirror above the washbasin.

He lay back in the bath. What a day. Then, as usually happened, elation gave way to fear. He was a man who'd lived for age, and age was now here. Even thirty years later, he still remembered the shock of recognition he'd felt on reading in Dante about those who'd made the great refusal and never truly lived. They were so insignificant and ignominious they were unworthy even of Hell and so ran round and round Inferno's outer wall in an endless train ('death had undone so many'), stung by hornets. They are me, Porlock thought. How would it all work out? In failure? Again? Remember 1962?

******

The bar was empty and smelling, as they all did, of brandy and water. He ordered a beer and sat at the counter. The barman stared, companionably, through the window unconsciously and expertly twisting a cloth inside a glass.

"You from England, Chief?" he asked Porlock suddenly.

Porlock nodded as he swallowed beer. "Yes," he said.

"Same here. Staying long?"

"Sailing tomorrow."

"I've been here since 1919."

"That's over forty years," Porlock calculated. "You haven't lost your accent."

"I'm a Cockney," said the barman proudly. "Cockneys never do." He picked up another glass and stared out of the window (which also needed cleaning). The ocean crashed on rocks not far away. Palm fronds like small explosions swayed in a hot breeze. "It was winter when I left," he said, again abruptly. "I'll never forget it. I stowed away."

"Oh, yes?"

"On a ship. It was all gaslight in them days, was London. Something chronic. Cold. Wet. Miserable. Not like here. I was fed up, you see. Just out of the Army and fed up."

"You'd been in Flanders?"

"Nah. They signed the Armistice, didn't they? Not that I minded. Not bleeding likely. Blimey, no. Being in the Army was bad enough." He finished polishing the glass and absent-mindedly picked up the one he'd already cleaned. Business was slack. Porlock was killing time. So was the barman. "'Selling cabbages off a barrer?' I says to my old man. 'Not me,' I says. 'I want more out of life than that,' I says. So he turns round and he says to me, he says: 'If you're so bleeding clever,' he says, 'get out of my house and find yourself a better hole.' 'I will,' I says. 'You see if I don't,' I says. 'See that you do,' he says, 'and don't come back.' 'Don't worry,' I says. 'I wouldn't be seen dead in a dump like this.' So that night I goes down to the docks and gets aboard the first ship what I sees. I was lucky, see, 'cos she sailed on the next tide. But, blimey, was I hungry? Was I ever. I stuck it out in the hold as long as I could and then I surfaced." He smiled, remembering. "Cor blimey, Chief, I'll never forget the Captain's face. A big ginger-haired bloke he was with side-whiskers and a temper to match. 'A stowaway,' he says. 'In my ship?' he says. 'I'll have no stowaways here, my lad. You'll get to work.'"

Calmly and professionally the barman switched glasses and went on polishing.

"And then?"Porlock prompted.

"Why, I got to work,' said the barman, surprised by the question. "Deck-hand, unpaid, but grub thrown in and a hammock down among the rats in the hold. But I was young in them days, see, and up for any lark. I'm a bit wiser and cuter now. Wilkinson. That were his name. Cap'n Wilkinson. I'll never forget him. 'If you're looking for adventure, my lad,' he says, 'you've come to the right place.'"

The barman broke off to serve a customer who came in out the heat. "Cold beer," the man ordered. (No women were allowed in bars in those days.) The barman snapped the cap off the beer bottle and handed it over. (Bottled beer, the only kind, was served glass-less in those old days.) Then he went back to staring out of the window and re-polishing the second – or was it the first? – glass.

"Well, what happened then?"

"Eh?"

"You'd stowed away. Remember? Looking for adventure. What happened next?"

"Why, I come here."

"Here?"

"Why, yes, *here*," said the barman. His finger indicated the big bar room they were in.

"Here? This bar?"

"Why, yes, here. Where else? Course, it's been done up a bit since, but it's the same old place underneath it all. I'm head barman now. Have been for fifteen years. Married. Had kids. Got grand-kids now. Funny thing, though," he added. "I never took out papers. Never got what you might call naturalised.

Always liked to think I had a place to go back to. Know what I mean, Chief?"

******

And Porlock did know. Know what the barman had meant. But what made him remember all that? He'd tried to cut out the past. The butterflies fluttered. What Butterfly Effect were they stirring up? Another defeat? But now he had no place to go back to. And anyway he couldn't fail. He had money enough for ten years and after that .....

CHAPTER 4

There was a curious stillness and peace about breakfast on the terrace in that perfect summer weather. The terrace had a squared-off concrete balustrade, painted white but blistered in places. Lavender, mint, rosemary, ivy, and even olive trees, grew in terracotta boxes and pots. Parasols, advertising Champagne, shut out the sun's direct light but not the sun glitter on the sea.

Porlock joined JJ who was reading the morning paper. "Have you noticed," said JJ, looking over the top of the broadsheet, "how many doctors are writing letters to the press these days?"

"Of philosophy or medicine?" Porlock queried

"Philosophy, I hope. Most of them are incredibly dim. You expect philosophers to be thick, but it's worrying when physicians are."

Porlock began with muesli, dried currants, red currants, figs, chocolate cornflakes, milk and yoghurt. A gull hopped from the concrete balustrade on to a table to peck at the butter dish. Then Porlock, before the marmalade and toast (which, for him, was what breakfast was really all about) ate a kipper. Should be feed the gull with the kipper skin? The waitress in a black waistcoat and tie stopped all thoughts of that. The coffee pots were still silver and, though battered, still capable of glaring with reflected sunlight fierce enough to leave and afterglow in the eyes.

Margot limped over to speak to them just as Joyce caught up with her. "Oh, Margot," she said. "Tomlinson's have been on the phone badgering again."

"Not again? After last time? And what about Mr Bradshaw? Have we heard from him lately?"

"Oh, my life! I'd forgotten about him. Not for a month or two."

"Are Tomlinson's still on the phone?"

"No, I got rid of them for the time being, thank goodness."

"Leave it with me, Joyce. I'll phone them later.

"I wish you would," said Joyce, walking back to reception.

"It's called aggressive marketing, Joyce," JJ called after her and then, to Margot: "Mr Bradshaw?"

"Oh, some old gent who thinks we have a painting which should rightly belong to him. He's never seen it and neither have I. His description of it is so vague, as well."

"Were you open during the war?" Porlock asked suddenly for no particular reason.

"No, we were requisitioned from the off. I was in the Wrens for most of the War. Ma was in Brambletown. We still have a couple of pill boxes. We should do something with them. What can we do with them, you two?"

"Mini-museums?" Porlock suggested.

"Exhibitions of camouflage," said JJ.

"Or both," Margot agreed.

After breakfast Porlock set off for a walking day out. On either side, stretched a switchback of hills and sea crags with a fringe of white surf. A westerly breeze was blowing. The sand bank was now hour-glass shaped isthmus: the sea on the western side was blue but filled with bay-shaped white crested waves: the eastern side was flat and green. Porlock walked between the two waters. up passed the car parks and the bungalows until he could turn west into the combe and the river which flowed down it.

The climb was steep and he took his time, stopping often. The sun was already burning on his right shoulder, neck and head. It was amazing – all that heat carried through the zero cold of space and it was still hot, more like mass than energy. The small of his back and shirt were soon wet.

Trees on the fringe of the wood were in the full glare of the late morning sun. The flat of the leaves which caught the light glinted like the sea. He stopped to gaze from one to the other, at sea sparkle and at leaf shine. No breeze moved either. A hayfield was ready for mowing, brought along by the recent hot sunshine. In his mind the scent of hay and the sound of wood doves were linked forever.

It was cooler in the woods: the coolness did what the heat couldn't – dried both skin and cloth. He followed the stream up through the trees until he crossed a path running along the contour of the hills. He walked on it for a couple of miles until he came to the bigger River Bramble. Sun shone in shafts through the late morning woods into the gullies. Moss on the oaks was still moist with last week's rain. The delicacy of the sorrel and stream-side buckle fern proved they didn't need to be robust in that benign place. Water endlessly coiled around rocks in the river, curling in eddies. Framed by an arch of leaves was a view of the bay, from Rumble Point to Bramble Head, with the whitewashed inn on its great stone sharp against the sea. The incoming tide had already turned the stone into an island again.

Porlock sat under an oak on a little knoll with a view of the sea. Margot had given him a packed lunch in a box which he'd carried in plastic shopping bag along with a small flask of tea. It was good place, the inn: he'd even been asked what he'd like in his sandwiches. Cheese and pickle, he'd said, and corned beef (his tastes were simple). There was also an apple, a piece of cake, and a small salad. He sat back contentedly: when alone he never felt lonely. A blackbird sang nearby and he thought he heard a yellow hammer. Surely not? It must have been fifty years ago since he'd last heard one.

Then time stopped and the world of solid places dematerialised, giving way to pure peace in a purity of nothingness. It often happened and could happen at the oddest times and in the strangest places. It happened once, he remembered, on the Isle of Dogs in 1965.....

..... In the pub, the noise was so loud it vibrated in his lungs. Just standing on the floor made his feet tingle. The noise came from a pop group – drummer, two guitarists, lead singer plugged into amplifiers as big as wardrobes – on a low stage lit by three red spotlights. They were belting out *Tobacco Road*. Worried that he'd go deaf, and feeling shrivelled up with loneliness, Porlock left when the noise rumbled into a kind of silence. It started again before he was outside: *My Poor Old-fashioned Baby*. He touched the wall of the pub – the bricks trembled and shook – before turning and walking off down the dark gaslit alley. He wore a duffle coat with a hood – the anorak of the nerds of his day. A band in the next pub played pre-war and wartime songs. There was a fish tank and a lot of matronly women filling the space behind the bar.

Then he walked along to the Thames and into the lift down to the foot tunnel. He was flat footed, rather slow and heavy, conscious of his footfalls. A few feet above his head the cold black muddy river poured down to the sea. The tunnel was white and tiled, spiralling on forever, splashed and shining with lights. He went up the lift on the other side, under the crossed yards of the *Cutty Sark*. "Well," he asked himself aloud, "where do you go from here?" Into the next pub, he decided. There was a pianist there, too, and a bar full of people singing.

"Pint of bitter, please," Porlock said.

"A pint, dear?"

"Please."

"What's the weather like out?" the man on the next stool asked him. "Snowing yet?"

"Not yet."

"I'm driving a ten ton lorry up to Hull on Monday. You don't want snow when you're doing that."

"No, you don't at that"

The pub got noisier, the singing louder. Tobacco smoke floated in layers. It was getting late though the landlord hadn't yet called time and the clock above the etched Victorian mirror was probably fast. He could stand the loneliness no longer: abruptly he stood up and edged and squeezed his way through the crowd into the street. Then he ran down to and through the foot tunnel, the skirts of his duffle coat banging against his knees, breath turning to steam in the clammy river-wet air and cold light. Above ground, it was snowing ....

It was then that it happened as it did nearly fifty years later in the woods overlooking the sea and as it had many times throughout the empty years in between. There was no simple way of saying what it was because whatever you said would be self-contradictory – like the base-less base of all that is. More understandably, it could be said to be the purity of peace below place and time.

He also knew what other people said it was since he'd read all the standard authors. Temperamentally, he was drawn to the 14th century German School of Eckhart and Ruysbroeck although at one time he'd been attracted to Zen because of the clarity of its thought and the concrete clarity of its art, particularly poetry. In the end, though, he decided Zen was too far from his own Greek-based civilisation, great as Japanese culture was. But even Eckhart was a bit too second-hand. Somewhere he had to find his own insight and (for reasons he couldn't explain) had begun with *Gideon's God* – without, of course, knowing the slightest thing about it. All the same, it would – he hoped – be his private Holy Grail.

He also knew that this strange experience came when thought was stopped – but only when he was alone. Company was deadly. So he wasn't too pleased by what happened that evening. He was sitting below the coloured glass dome of the Palm Court reading the menu. He, having been a teetotaller for twenty five years, had already ordered tomato juice.

"Hello!"

He looked up.

"Hello," the lady repeated. "We meet again."

"Hello," he replied, a bit puzzled. The woman who stood in front of him was a little on the short side, a little plump, and large breasted. Her hair, almost but not quite shoulder length, was cut to frame a face which, though care-worn, was still attractive.

"You don't remember me, do you?" she said with a note of alarm.

Only vaguely, Porlock thought. Then: "Yes, of course, you're the lady of the quay", glamorised and done up the nines, he added to himself.

"Key with a 'k'?"

"Quay with a 'q'. Yesterday."

"May I join you?"

"Well, yes, I suppose so," said Porlock reluctantly, moving his glass much as she'd moved her cup yesterday.

"I was in a B&B with two old dears who hogged the bathroom. I thought I'd try a little luxury for a change."

"Bit run down here, isn't it, for luxury?"

"Nice enough," she said. "Did you find *Aaron's Rod*?"

"*Gideon's God*," he corrected her. "Not yet. It's deep in the chambers of this rock, somewhere. Margot's still looking." He pointed through the window. "See that hut-like thing? That's the outside entrance – sealed off to us to paying punters – to the caves and chambers. There's another door in the wine cellar which the staff use. The painting's down there somewhere."

"It is a painting then?"

"Yes."

"May I ask you your name?" When she saw Porlock hesitate, she said quickly: "I'm Catherine Finch."

"Porlock."

"Is that your Christian name?"

"Surname."

"Lord Porlock? Don't you have a first name?"

"Not one that I use much. Not if I can help it."

"What is it then?"

"Well, it's … erm … well, Joshua, actually."

"Oh, but it's a lovely name. Your mother must have liked it."

"She didn't give it me."

"Oh?"

"She died in childbirth. Or very soon after."

"Oh," said Mrs Finch. "I'm sorry."

"Long time ago."

"Why don't you call me Kate?" said Mrs Finch after a long pause.

"Kate? Yes, all right."

"And tell me who called you Joshua."

"You don't remember the War?"

"Do I look that old?"

"No, no, of course not."

"Is your name to do with the War?"

"Well, yes. It was a bit of wartime black humour, I suppose. Apparently, we lived in a block of Peabody Dwellings called Jericho. There was a direct hit in the next street."

"And the walls came tumbling down?"

"It killed my mother."

"The midwife called you Joshua?"

"Or somebody in the hospital. Or orphanage. You do ask a lot of questions."

"I'm so sorry."

"What for?" (Not for asking impudent questions, he thought, annoyed with himself for giving so much away.)

The waiter came over. Kate asked for a gin and tonic.

"May I join you for dinner, Joshua?"

"Well, yes, I suppose so," said Porlock, thinking she was becoming a bloody nuisance.

"May I call you Joss?"

"Well, yes, I *suppose* so," said Porlock, so convinced of it that his exasperation was showing.

CHAPTER 5

Flashback: May 2004

One morning back in late May, Freddie Maddox had stood on the harbour-side in the sunshine before the start of that long heat wave, though of course he hadn't known that. His café tables had been filling nicely, his tills likewise, mid-morning pastries were already selling well: Cornish pasties and cream teas would be selling later in the day. He'd taken out his mobile phone, run down through the menu and pressed 'send'. "Gabriel?"

"Hello, Freddie, my old china, and how's the great art robbery going?"

"Bit of hitch this end, Gabie. A hiccup, really, but something you should be able to sort out."

"Tell Uncle Gabriel all about it, then, Freddie."

"Our villain at this end wants a bit of help from a villain on the inside."

"I see," said Gabriel, "so your bloke is now the get-away driver?"

"There's a reason for it, Gabe. A technical one. The hired help will have be presentable, of course. No striped jerseys and bag labelled 'swag'."

"A Raffles look alike, you mean," said Gabriel.

"Isn't that a hotel in Singapore? Chota pegs and mem-sahibs, that kind of thing."

"Also a gentleman-crook, Freddie. Useful batsman and accomplished jewel thief."

"Can you lay hands on somebody like him?"

"What's the plan, Freddie?" Freddie told him in some detail.

"Not too risky, is it?" Gabriel asked when he'd finished.

"Not in the right hands."

"Let me have a word with a man who knows a man."

Freddie looked at the sun glint on the water. "By the way, Gabriel," he said at length, "just how bent is our friendly solicitor?"

"As a fish hook, old boy."

"Can we trust him?'

"I was going to phone you about him. He's got a bee in his bonnet about the old biddy down there hanging on to a daub that rightfully belongs to him. Would you oblige by half-inching it on his behalf?"

"Oh, for God's sake, Gabriel, haven't we got enough on our plates?"

"I think the old boy's going gaga – delusions of grandeur and all that. But you're going to have to lift at least half a dozen to make it look like a job lot and not a bit of larceny to order."

"No promises, Gabriel. From what I can make out, it's chaos in those cellars."

"I'll get a description of the picture old Bradshaw wants and let you know. Meanwhile I'll sort out Raffles for you."

"You'll let me know soon?"

"Give me an hour. Max." In fact it was two. "We have our man, Freddie. Name of Jeremy Green. Not exactly well-bred but he can put on a bit of an act, apparently. Never done porridge, semi-retired on the Costa del Crime somewhere. In other words, he knows his stuff."

"Sounds pricey."

"He is."

"It's worth the outlay?"

"Chalk it up to expenses."

"Oh, yeah, the Inland Revenue would love that."

"Bread on the water, Freddie, old bean. Bread on the water. And besides, soon it'll be loose change."

"Send him down then, Gabe. In for a penny in for a bloody pound." Freddie had hung up and lit one of his cigarillos. He'd looked at the sun glinting on the harbour water and then, more approvingly, at the punters busily ordering Danish pastries and croissants, all with low fat content, all with nice high mark ups.

CHAPTER 6

Wednesday was another picture-free day and one which, if Porlock could help it, was going to be Kate-free as well. Today he went east around the curve of the sand to the Beacon Head. He'd always been elated when setting out to discover what was on the other side of the hill, across the river or in the next valley. Walking was easy on the hard sand by the sea. Under the Head the going got harder among slippery rocks and a network of rock pools, but it was grand, in his words, to be under the dark stone cliff with its scent and sense of pre-human time: Porlock often felt rooted in ancient rocks.

Beyond the hard place was a bay of soft sand dunes and beyond that a sphagnum bog. A camping and caravan site stretched in a long line along the hillside above them. Millions of footfalls had trodden a gully through the dunes: roots of marram grass hung down forlornly like bundles of tangled string. Duckboards now led over the flat inland part of the dunes. Flights of plank stairs carried people over the sand hills and down on the beach. Bog and dunes were now Nature Reserves with a guardian warden, a botanist who also ran guided tours. Porlock tagged along at the back of one. The duckboards, she explained, were to keep people off the sand to allow the wind to fill in a particularly deep gully which holiday makers' feet had eroded almost to bed rock. The tour took in a creeping willow (a tree as flat as any mat and only six inches tall), sea spurge, bird's foot trefoil, orchids, blue butterflies and frogs as yellow as sand. In the distance Porlock spotted JJ labouring down to the shore with an easel, boxed paints, and his tobacco tinged beard, toes snagging in the gaps between the slats of the duckboards. He was heading for coffee in the Warden's shack. When the tour was over, the Warden went back there too.

******

"Morning, Warden," JJ greeted her. "How's the wound?"

"Mine or the dunes?" asked Tilly.

"Yours first."

"Unhealing, Jay."

"You need a lover, my handsome."

"I'd opt for asexual. Never mind, the sea's beautiful today. I've never seen it so green. Does it have a name, that colour?"

"Malachite, I'd say. Or guess. It's not an exact science, the naming of colours, unlike botany. Not a good a name, though, is it? Malachite? A bit too Biblical. Smite the Malachites, O Lord, smite them hip and thigh."

Tilly plugged in a kettle in one corner and set about making coffee, instant, in gaudy mugs. "I love your painting of the dunes before the trippers eroded that gully through them," she told him over her shoulder. "When was that? Back in the '50s?"

"It was a kind of therapy, you know. After the war."

"JJ, I didn't know. I didn't think you looked old enough."

"All us old buggers had our wars, Till. Mine's damn near forgotten now. Korea. Remember that?"

"Only very vaguely."

"The Imjin River?"

"No. Sorry."

Tilly's hut had views of both the sea and the dunes. The gully was nearly filled in but still dipped distinctively into a col on the ridge. It took him back to the little saddle among the scrubby bushes below the low peak on the hill by the 38th parallel. The Imjin flowed through a moonscape of low mounds in a flat valley, its course marked by bulbous trees. A bright invaders' road cut across in a straight and shining line. That night the enemy came. Guns seized up with the heat of firing. In the hut by the wounded dunes JJ looked away to the clean sea but in its flash and sparkle he saw again the drum-major lit by gun fire in the otherwise dark of the night playing regimental tunes on a bugle. The battalion held – it was all it had to do – but men died by the hundred and very few rode out on the tanks of the Hussars when they were ordered to withdraw.

"Jay? JJ? Penny for them?"

"Oh, nothing, Till. Just a few forgotten far off things and a battle long ago. If, that is, I'm quoting the old boy correctly."

"Bad was it?"

"No, not really. Do you remember the otter man? Maxwell?"

"*Ring of Bright Water*?"

"At the time I thought of going to the West Highlands like he did. He went off to where the sea was clean. To cleanse himself, I suppose. In my case it was also human meat. We drove over them in the tanks when we broke out. The tracks were clogged."

"Oh, God, but that's awful, JJ. That's terrible. I just never realised."

"Long time ago, Tilly. Turned me into a painter, though. My way of cleaning the mind."

"Is that what art's for, do you think?"

"Some old bloke once said all good art creates a 'point of rest'."

"What does bad art do?"

"Creates a 'point of unrest', logically. That's what I believe. Probably nobody else does. Nobody living, that is, and as far as I know. A few dead'uns believed it but since they're worth more than all the living put together, I take a fair bit of comfort from that. In the end you can't live by what other people think, can you? And we live in such conformist times."

"John J Jordan you really are a terrible old reactionary."

"I know, I know. I try to conform, Tilly Girl, I really do, but reality keeps on breaking in. It must have been the way my mother put my hat on."

"What?"

"Old saying, Tilly. God knows what it means. You should take up painting. Paint a wound to heal a wound?"

"No, thank you, JJ, he's a pretty naff sort of bloke. A broom and two buckets of whitewash are all I'd need."

"As long as it's not bile yellow. Bitterness is such a terrible killer."

When he'd finished his coffee, JJ put on a wide brimmed hat, picked up his folding stool, and went looking for a spot to set up his easel. He'd painted the dunes fifty years ago, before they'd been eroded, and now he wanted to do the same again in the same place – now facing the gully and the duckboards which bridged it.

37

******

By now Porlock, strolling eastward, had reached the sphagnum bog. They said it bounced like a water bed if you jumped on. Porlock did, having checked he was alone. The bog not only bounced, it squelched and sucked up cold water to wet his shoes. He was alone again, gazing across a flat circle of moss covered rain water between the hills and the sea. Not a soul was in sight. Wonderful: he wished he could stay there alone forever, just standing stock still. Then he roused himself and went looking for the candy-striped caterpillars of the Rosy Marsh Moth but failed to find one. There were a few blue dragonflies, not yet mated, and sundews which kept their mouths open for flies. The moss, he'd read, was good as an anti-septic dressings and had been so used in the Great War.

Duckboards criss-crossed the whole bog also. He walked along one to the centre. The bog, a good quarter of a mile across, was fringed by alders and the horizon of the sea. He stood in the hot silence of a summer's afternoon and absorbed and was dissolved by time and space. Who was the absorbed, what the absorber?

******

Meanwhile, JJ worked steadily for three or so hours before going back to Tilly's hut, which was also the Reserve's information centre, to share a sandwich with her and talk to tourists. They sat together on the covered veranda overlooking the sea. Inside, maps, photographs and diagrams were pinned to a series of free standing notice boards, explaining the work of the Reserve. Then, in the afternoon, JJ worked for another couple of hours, the heat of the day almost drying the paint on his brushes. Some people stopped to watch, mostly they crossed the duckboard bridge to flop on the beach on the other side of the dunes. The tide turned: the sand shrank.

JJ had just packed up when Porlock came back from the sphagnum bog. He helped him carry his easel and paints up over the duckboards to where his car was parked on the caravan site. It was a small red Fiat. "Chosen because it's Italian," JJ explained. "No other reason. Except it was going cheap." He also drove like an Italian – fast, braking hard on bends, scraping by oncoming traffic. "How's your no-claims bonus?" Porlock asked him.

"Intact, oddly enough. Does my driving bother you?"

"Well, it's exhilarating, to say the least."

"Margot is less polite and a damned sight more earthy. Downright Anglo-Saxon, in fact. Don't know where she can have learned words like them."

"Did you know Mr and Mrs Margot?"

"Ma Montague, yes. There never was a Pa Montague. Margot's mother always said she never knew who the father was."

"You sound a bit doubtful, JJ."

"Well, yes, I am, frankly. I first met old Ma Montague when she was still quite young, still relatively unchanged by age, and there was no real resemblance between mother and daughter. To me, that suggests Margot just might take more after her father. And if that's true, then Ma Montague must have sussed out who papa was at some stage."

"It's never bothered Margot, though? Not knowing who her father was, I mean."

"At one time perhaps. But Margot must be nearly eighty – *over* eighty just about, and things don't matter much when you get that old."

JJ jerked the car down into the lane between the new bungalows to the ferry, braking finally outside the hotel's private car park. He leaned out to key in the code to open the gate. Together they carried the gear to the sea tractor. A younger man drove it.

They carried the gear into the cool reception area and stacked it near the desk. Joyce was checking in a guest. "My dear life," she called over, "you looked frazzled out, both of you. Don't you go overdoing it."

"You boys look as though you need a drink," Margot greeted them. "Come along." They followed her to the old Palm Court and sat in Lloyd Loom wickerwork chairs by a Lloyd Loom wickerwork table. From there they they had a perfect panoramic view of the cliffs reaching to the far eastern headland which Porlock had walked around that morning. A waiter appeared immediately. "What are you having?" Margot asked them,

"Something stiff enough to take my mind off this damned

arthritis, Margot, if you don't mind. Like an old fool, I've been doing a bit of scrabbling over the dunes." That something turned out to be a large whisky and a small soda, Margot asked for a small white house wine, Porlock ordered mineral water.

"Did you paint the damage to the dunes, JJ?" Margot began when the waiter had gone. "I'd like to hang it alongside the old one on Saturday, even if it isn't quite finished."

"It isn't quite right or ready, Margot. Perhaps a label to say it's unfinished? What reputation I have needs protecting."

"Your reputation can take a few knocks, JJ, but yes of course a little notice. How badly damaged are the dunes at the moment? I can't get over there so easily these days, you know," she added as an aside to Porlock.

"They're becoming pretty un-damaged," JJ answered. "Strange the power of duckboards and a brisk sea breeze. How do you un-damage people, though, Margot? Can you tell me that?"

"Love, my old Ma always said, and she would have known if anybody did. She certainly practised what she preached."

"As I recall, Margot, you were a bit of a goer yourself in the old days."

Porlock jerked upright, shocked. Margot noticed. "Don't mind, JJ," she said. "And any way it's no secret in these parts."

"And, I suspect, Mr Porlock gave up being shocked forty years ago. Like the rest of us. Isn't that right?"

"Thirty years ago, JJ. I was a late developer," Porlock answered untruthfully. He was easily shocked, easily put out, easily shut up by slights.

"My Ma really did love 'em all," Margot went on. "With me there was only ever the one."

"Well, you can't pump love out of the ground like oil, can you?"

"No, thank God," said Margot. "Can you imagine what the nannies in this Government would do?"

"It'd be illegal by now," JJ almost laughed. (Laughing made him cough so he did as little of it as possible.) "Or taxed."

The waiter came back with the drinks on a tray. He placed them carefully, on coasters, smiled and left them alone again.

"I liked your story about the artist who painted God, by the way," said JJ. "What was his name again?"

"Comely," Margot said. "Gideon. Gideon Comely."

"What do we know about him?'

"Hardly anything, I'm ashamed to say. Do you, Joshua?"

"Absolutely nothing. Just the name and the name of the painting."

"I think he may have been a very damaged man but why I think that I'm not sure. If he were, it could have been because of the Great War. Are you damaged, JJ?"

"Not any more, my old love. For me, art's been the great healer. Art's a kind of love, isn't it? Or should it. What it is today, God only knows."

"I've always thought so," Margot agreed. Two sparrows quarrelled and hopped in the vetch outside. She looked at them for a moment. "There is something else I seem to remember about Mr Comely," Margot hesitated. "I think he may have shot himself."

"My God!" Porlock exclaimed, truly shocked.

"That's a shame," JJ said, reflectively. "It puts the kibosh on my theory about art the healer, don't you think?"

"Perhaps not," Margot replied. "I have a feeling he gave it up and stopped painting. There was talk of a bonfire of canvases on the sand in the bay out there – long before the last War, that was. They could have been his, I suppose."

"If what you suppose is right," said Porlock, "then *Gideon's God* down in the cellar is all that's left of him."

The thought dried up conversation for a while. The Palm Court, like the rest of the inn, was now a bit tatty. At one time a white baby grand piano had stood in the corner, after the fashion of the 1930s, but no more. A fountain with a black mosaic pool – black, gold, blue tesserae – still played, occasionally. It was decorated with a vaguely ancient Egyptian pattern of palm fronds – the kind slaves might have waved to cool a pharaoh. Marble steps led up to the Sun Lounge, a semi-circular room under a semi-circular glass roof. Then Joyce came over with a copy of the inventory, and sat down. "I've been thinking, my lovers." She ticked a line in the inventory and handed the paper to Margot.

"Would that be Mr Bradshaw's picture?" she asked.

"I think so."

"'Tis among the missing ones."

"Yes?"

"Between ourselves – what if Mr Bradshaw has stole it?"

"Stolen it?"

"Had it stole, then. They took Mr Porlock's with the other half dizzen to put us off the scent." JJ and Margot looked doubtful. "'Tisn't likely the paintings clopped off on their own," Joyce argued triumphantly. "If they're not here, 'tis coz they've been took."

"There's still one more place to look, Joyce. We haven't given up all hope yet."

CHAPTER 7

Flashback: 1983

By 1983, Mrs Kitty Bradshaw had scant hair, swollen ankles, and walked with a stick. She was moving into sheltered housing not far from the island. Her son, sleek, portly and around fifty, was there to see her settled – and off his hands. To his surprise, she'd asked him to phone the hotel and ask if they could visit the ball room for a few minutes. The ball room's dancing days were also over – it had been locked and unused for years. But, obligingly, a much younger Margot unlocked the double doors, and pushed down the gilded handles.

"We won't be more than a few minutes," Mrs Bradshaw told her.

"I'll leave you alone then. "

"Thank you." Drawn curtains filtered and softened the hot afternoon light. Thin shafts of sunshine broke through here and here to and lit up single strands of cobwebs. "Reggie," she said when Margot had gone. "There's something I want to tell you."

"Why here?"

"This is where I met your father."

"I thought you met in Macclesfield."

"Not George Bradshaw."

"Who then?"

"His name was Reggie Kettlethorpe."

"Not that old fossil in the House of Lords?"

"He died last month."

"But my *father*?"

"He was a hero in the war, even if he was too old for the call-up."

"But he deserted you. He deserted me, come to that."

"*You've* never gone short, have you?"

"Did Dad know?"

"He wasn't much cop as a revolutionary, wasn't Georgie

Bradshaw. More like a weathervane. Oh, yes, he knew all right – knew which side his bread was buttered."

"I had no idea. No idea at all."

"Well, I wasn't going to blab, was I? And then your … and then George Bradshaw died suddenly."

"And you conceived me *here*. *Here*, of all places?"

"Well, Room fifty-three, to be exact. This ballroom was a bit crowded at the time. But we met here. It was a wonderful summer. Such a very wonderful summer."

"But, mother …."

"Yes, Reggie?"

"I'm a solicitor …."

"Yes, Reggie, I'm well aware of that but back then that dry legal brain of yours wasn't around to advise me."

"All I can is I'm dumbstruck. Dumbfounded. I mean, I don't know what to say. What can I say?"

"How about 'how could you?'"

"Yes, well, how could *you*?"

"Well, it was all very easy as it happens. He turned out to be a good man in the end as well. And who'd have thought that? He was such a soppy toff back then. But I loved him so much. The only man I've ever loved. Still do. Funny, isn't it? We don't have choices when it comes to falling it love, do we? Not that you ever have."

"Mother?"

"*Yes, Reggie*, what is it now?"

"What about the title?"

"What about it?"

"Did he have another son?"

"No. Plenty of nephews, though."

"What number was he in the line of succession?"

"Eleventh."

"*Eleventh*? Oh, my God! By rights, I'm the twelfth Earl of Kettlethorpe."

"No, Reggie, you aren't. We had a photo taken here while we danced. I wonder what became of that? There was a painting too, so your … so Lord Kettlethorpe told me later."

"By rights, I should be in Parliament making the law, not just practising it."

"No, Reggie. You don't practise the law, you break it. Don't think I don't know what you get up to."

When that shut him up, she went on: "What a wonderful summer that was, what a truly wonderful summer, the summer of 1923."

CHAPTER 8

June 2004

Thursday was for walking all over the island – all thirty? forty? (fifty at the most?) acres of it.

It was an odd patch of land, like two different places stuck together: the landward side was sandy, soft and accessible. Yukkas grew in place of palms. The seaward end was ringed by black and sharply bladed rocks (stone was too soft a word for them) leaning menacingly over. At least six coves were cut out of that southern coast, all but one were gashes of black rock and seething water where no boat could land.

On the mainland, the long line of cliffs rose and fell like regular waves reaching to the far horizon. If the sea moved at short-wave lengths, the land was energy of the long-wave kind. The cliffs and the hinterland behind them were covered with green grass, grazed in great fields by flocks of sheep no bigger than dots. It was a day of distance and salt-laden sea-haze. The far headland was misty-grey in the sun-stained sea. 'The Apple Isle of Avalon is out there to the west,' Porlock – the romantic – thought.

Landscape, not people, was nature's gift to Porlock. People he misunderstood: people misunderstood him. In fact, he'd always felt he was an alien from another planet – at one time, quite literally: in his later twenties, he refused to see a doctor when he'd been very ill because he was convinced his body was so different that no diagnosis was possible, not to a human physician any way. The untreated sickness – possibly pneumonia – had scarred his lungs: climbing hills or stairs always left him breathless from that day to this. He wheezed now as the laboured up to the summit and the ruins of the huer's hut. He remembered reading about huers many years ago (everything he knew seemed to come out of a book): "In season, pilchards stained the sea for miles. Each village employed a 'huer' to keep a lookout and raise the cry when a shoal was sighted. The oil was pressed out in pilchard cellars. Many of the pressed fish – now called fairmaids (fumadoes) – were exported to southern Europe." The entry (in a guide book, he seemed to remember) went on to describe the presses and the gurries (or wheelbarrows) used in the cellars. "Pilchards disappeared – quite suddenly and probably from natural causes – around 1916".

History of that kind, rather than living people, appealed to him. But most of all, it was landscape which stretched the skin of this world to let through a glimmer of another place a Great Elsewhere – of unspoilable happiness. Landscape was like a catalyst or enzyme making it happen, but not itself part of the result.

For it to happen at all, he needed to be alone and at no time in his life had that been a problem. Except now, looking down from the crest of the island, he saw Mrs Finch climbing inexorably upwards to disturb the one thing he'd always lived for. What was wrong with the woman? Kate, panting slightly, joined him on top of the hill. She wondered about the roofless one-room stone house with paneless windows in each of its four walls, and fireplace with a narrow chimney. He told her about fairmaids and pilchards, fish presses and gurries. She seemed interested.

"Any news of your painting?" she asked as they walked along the crest of the one-hill island. So he told her about Joyce's latest theory. They stood looking down on the inn and, to its left, the pub down by the shore. "I hope you won't be disappointed?" she said. "You've never said why it's so important to you."

"Well, for one thing, I don't know. I don't even know where I heard about it. I think I read it in a book, thirty, forty, years ago but which book it was I've completely forgotten. It isn't part of the Gutenberg Project and has never been digitalised. He's not in Wikipedia. Google's never heard of him. Not that it would matter if they did. It was no more than a passing reference to something called *Gideon's God* and that it was down in this neck of the woods. Somehow, it seemed important to me. Well, to be honest, I tossed a coin. A pound one. Heads, here, tails think again. Any way, this is as good a place as any to start. Better than most. The best, the way things are working out. I love it here."

"But you'll be disappointed if it's lost?"

"Haunted, might be a better word. Who is Gideon? What happened to him? Did he burn his work? Did he stop painting altogether? Are his paintings in a vault somewhere, like Margot's little collection? Why did he want to paint God? How can you paint God? Did he have a special insight or what?"

"You're investing too much in him, Joss. Wouldn't he be better known if he were any good?"

"I suppose so. That's the theory and probably the usual reality. But perhaps he's unknown because only that one painting survived. We just don't know."

Going downhill was harder than climbing – harder on ageing knees. They followed a path with steps so deep they almost had to climb down them. But at the bottom, they found themselves outside the pub. The pub was pure delight to Porlock: purely Medieval with no additions – a re-materialised 14th century fisherman would have found little changed: potatoes and tobacco would take him aback but baguettes and lager were only variations on a well-known theme. The inn was sheltered by the rise of hill, otherwise its sign would have creaked in the wind on wild nights. As it was, it reminded Porlock of Billy Bones whose old age was blighted by Blind Pugh's Black Spot but who in turn terrorised the Benbow Inn, somewhere on a Cornish cliff which was, in all probability, not unlike the ones across the sand.

The pub was crowded with day trippers but Kate found two seats at one of the tables-cum-benches on the terrace overlooking the low tide sea. Sparrows fought noisily in the eaves. The sand isthmus, clear of water, shone golden yellow in the hot sunshine. To the east, the beach was getting crowded. Wind surfers and those with kite-powered boards criss-crossed the bay.

At first, as he stepped inside, Porlock was too sun-blinded to see a thing: the windows were small and the place as dark as a deep cave. Then, through the fading afterglow, he made out rough tables with lit candles, benches and settles, even an alcove half shut off from the other two rooms. The massive iron-grated fireplace was empty in this summer weather. Heavy beams held up the wooden planks of the ceiling. All the timber was black with age and tobacco smoke, though men had been drinking there long before tobacco arrived with Raleigh from the New World. For hundreds of years, he thought, men drinking ale or cider could have looked out of those tiny square windows at cogs and carracks, caravels and clippers, ships of the line, frigates under sail, destroyers emitting coal smoke, and more latterly at coasters and liners, aircraft carriers and tankers on the far horizon. Four feet of stone stood between drinkers and the outside world.

Kate and Porlock shared a ham and tomato baguette. A Medieval fisherman – or monk (the huer's was once the site of a monastery) – would have recognised ham and bread however strangely shaped, but what of the bright red tomato? Back then, it still only grew in the New World, then unknown even to exist. Kate also drank half a pint of Australian lager. Australia would have astonished – but lager? Or would that have been a variant on common ale and small beer?

The rest of the day they spent together. Kate was proving to be a sharp but homely companion, readily amused and fond of laughing and – even the people-blind Porlock began to suspect – unaccountably fond of him also. (What was there to be fond of?) Late in the afternoon, they parted to shower and change. Porlock was down first and joined JJ in the Palm Court.

After a few minutes, Margot walked over. "Oh, dear," she said, "I'm afraid we've been maligning poor old Mr Bradshaw. We've found the painting he wanted. Would you like to see it? It's in the ballroom."

It was propped against the wall, a space above all ready for its hanging. They were looking at a lean and sinuous young woman in a cloche hat dancing with a young man in a broadly, and brightly, striped blazer. His hair was parted down the middle and his face was the kind which – Wooster-like – once attracted monocles: his hadn't but it was wearing a rather soppy smile.

"Are they at a ball?" asked the unworldly Porlock.

49

"A tea-dance. We used to hold them in the afternoon. That window in the painting is the same one as the real window next to it. See?"

"Ah, yes," said Porlock, looking from painting to window, "so it is."

"We had to switch a few pictures around to get the real window and the painted window together. Janice calls it Post-Structuralist irony, whatever that means."

"Painted from a photograph,"JJ said after looking at it closely. "Who's that Scottish feller with the Italian name? He made a mint from paintings like that."

"Dancing on the sea shore," said Porlock.

"Yes, and a serving wench with a brolly. Corny stuff, but sellable. This would be also, Margot."

"No doubt. We have a ready-made buyer in Mr Bradshaw if we need one. But I'd rather keep Ma's collection together. I don't know why Mr Bradshaw can't be satisfied with a reproduction. It's not like the artist is famous. In fact, I don't who he was at all."

"If you've found the missing Earl," Porlock suggested, "perhaps Gideon's still down there in the dungeon?"

"Joshua, I do hope so."

CHAPTER 9

JJ wasn't on the terrace for breakfast on Friday morning, the last before the gallery opened. Porlock was finishing his muesli, dried currants, red currants, figs, chocolate cornflakes, milk and yoghurt. when Kate joined him. Afterwards, while Kate went back to her room, Porlock wandered into the ball room, soon to be called The Ball Room Gallery. Margot was there with Janice and another, much younger, woman. "Come in, Mr Porlock," Margot invited. "It's all girly talk in here, but you're welcome to stay. You know Janice, of course. And this young student person is Alice. She's here to help us."

Alice said hello. So did Porlock. "We haven't got your Gideon, Joshua," Margot went on. "We've looked everywhere and it just can't be found. Six other pictures are missing too"

"But this island is like a fortress," Porlock objected. "How could anybody smuggle six canvases ashore. Under their arms?"

"Well," Margot explained, "the chambers do connect to a tunnel which opens out on to a beach."

"*Gideon's God*, in'it?" Alice butted in. "Maybe the vicar stole it."

"Hardly," said Janice. "The vicar's a colour-blind atheist."

Porlock, who was fascinated by hidden spaces, asked her: "How many underground rooms are there?"

"Oh." Margot looked vague. "Several, really," she said in the end, obviously having failed to add them all up.

"In the rock itself?"

"Yes, like caves, only most of them aren't natural."

"No?"

"No. One was begun by the Tudors, we think. Perhaps they had in mind something like St Mawes. If they did it never came to anything. Others are Napoleonic, aren't they, Margot?" Janice continued. "Then there's some from the 1860s for reasons that escape me at the moment."

"And the Army added one or two in the last War. We found empty ammunition boxes in one of them."

"Are they dry? Is the temperature stable"

"Perfectly," Margot answered. "The inn's on top of them and the roof's on top of the inn, and it doesn't leak. Not yet, anyway."

"It's like a cave system." Janice explained. "It *is* a cave system."

"Have you ever thought of cave paintings?" Porlock suggested

"No," Margot admitted. "It might be a nice idea."

"What about concerts?"

"Not big enough for that. We're not Gibraltar, you know."

"Is the inventory accurate?" Porlock went off on another tack.

"My Ma made it out. I just don't think she'd have written down six non-existent paintings. One perhaps but not half a dozen."

"Is there a description?" Porlock asked. "I'd settle for that."

"Unfortunately, no. I suppose Ma knew what they all looked like and didn't think of it. And as far as I remember, I've never seen it."

"The police?"

"I've notified them. For all the interest they took. The sergeant's ears pricked when he heard about the local TV stations who're coming. Hopefully."

"Have you ever thought of video-art?" Alice chipped in.

Porlock wandered off as the three women took a break: the younger two stood with coffee cups in front of the work of the 1920s and '30s. Margot sat on a chair.

"Some years ago," Janice said. "I went up to London to look at the Turner prize finalists. One young woman had put a roll of fluff in a clear plastic box. What on earth is it? I asked her. She said it asks questions about the futility of life while exploring decay in new and challenging ways. I could hear the hoover jokes before she'd finished."

"Well, it was, like, conceptual, wasn't it?" Alice explained. "I mean most of these paintings don't ask any questions at all, do they?"

"Perhaps that's because they're answers," said Margot. "We can all ask questions, not many of us know the answers, though, do we?" She stood up a little laboriously. "Come here, will you Alice, please," she said, "and look at this."

"*Portrait of a Young Woman*? Manley Bingley? Who 'e, Margot?"

"He was a young man, Alice, and in this painting he's telling you something that you, as a woman, can never find out for yourself: how a woman looks to a man who loves her."

"Isn't she beautiful, though?" Janice remarked. "And so happy, too. How old do you think she is?"

"Eighteen."

"You knew her, then, Margot? Was it painted here?"

"No, it was wartime then. The Army had taken over the island."

"I bet she ended up as a housewife with, like, one of those skirts splayed out with petticoats and two point one kids and a fitted kitchen," Alice decided. And added: "With a hoover. So 1950s."

"No, Alice, he was killed in the War. I never married."

"Oh, Margot, you tricked us. That's, like, so unfair. You've changed so much how could we know?"

"Alice, do shut up. Margot, I'm so sorry. He must have thought the world of you, judging by the picture."

"I thought the world of him as well, Janice. People used to say Manley's mother forgot to look into the crystal ball when she called him Manley. And he always did seem a bit limp to others. But he wasn't. More distracted and other worldly."

"Can you ever tell which two people are suited to each other?"

"It's, like, all to do with pheromones, isn't it?" said Alice.

"Phera-what?"

"*Mones*. Smells. The way we smell."

"As a theory it lacks a certain something, Alice, don't you think?" Janice laughed. "*Ode to Body Odour*? It'll never catch on."

"Nobody can buck science, Janice, not even old romantics like you."

"At one time I thought of writing a book about all the

couples who've stayed in this inn," Margot went on. "I was going to call it *A Gathering Of Strangers*, because that's what most of them were to each other."

"Well," said Janice, "*I* was going to say that in the end nothing matters but love, but our one-woman anti-romance campaign here would only be rude about it."

"Well, no, Janice, it's just that blokes today are better at leavin' than lovin'. The good 'uns have, like, all gone – if there ever were any."

"Oh, there were, Alice. There certainly were. One or two, at least."

Kate came into the gallery at that moment. She immediately went over to Porlock. He was standing in front of a science fiction-like painting of a bright yellow sea and a dark red coastline with a red and yellow sky. Margot and Janice exchanged glances. Porlock didn't notice. Kate did, and didn't care.

CHAPTER 10

Next morning, Jake the ferryman made the first crossing of the day a little earlier than usual. It was opening day. He sat in the inn's private kitchen and ate breakfast with half a pint of sugared tea. The kitchen windows looked over the uncovering sand of the bay to the hedged and farmed hills beyond. The cliffs themselves were like changing paintings, a different colour as day, light, and the weather (mist, heat wave, sea spray) changed and went from marble-like white to khaki brown or a hazy blue.

"I hope you're going to be very busy today, Jake," Margot said, joining him. She'd already been up for a couple of hours. "Goodness knows we've distributed enough leaflets and posters, not to mention the radio talks. We've got the local TV people coming this morning, too. So just you look smart in case they want a picture of you."

"You know what it'll mean, don't you, Margot?" he told her gravely while pouring tea into his saucer: Jake, too, kept to country ways. "More grockles, that's what. *Grockles*. Just you mark my words, girl." He drank from his full saucer with a slight slurping sound.

"Grockles pay the ferryman, Jake. No grockles, no inn, no inn, no ferryman."

"Time was it was painters, painters, painters. Tattoos is the nearest grockles get to painting."

"I swear to God, Jacob Jewell, you get grumpier with every passing day."

"Entitled to. At my age."

"Jake, I can give you a good fifteen years," she replied good humouredly. "More than that, I can remember the very day you were born. Right here in the inn. Room twenty-three, the one Mr Porlock's in now. Two guests complained about the noise you were making. We haven't clapped eyes on either of them since. By rights I should sue you for loss of trade."

"How long can we all carry on?" Jake asked, suddenly

55

serious. "My old pins are getting too stiff to bend. Yours must be worse."

"I just wish I'd had children, or my old Ma had had more. A niece to leave things to would be nice. Keep it in the family. Over a hundred years now, isn't it, Jake, in one family? Yours isn't far behind."

"I'm surprised your Ma didn't have more, the way she carried on. She were a bowerly party in her day. A swinger, too, and no mistake."

"She was, Jake."

"Good days, too."

"Yes, Jake, they were good days."

"Upset they Wesleyans."

"We've been lucky."

******

At the same time across the bay, Janice was getting ready to leave for the day. She lived with her daughter and husband, Freddie Maddox, behind Anson's Restaurant which he both owned (leasehold) and managed. Freddie was in his dressing gown, still unshaved.

"Who was that man you were entertaining last night?" Janice asked him.

"Gino? Nobody for you to concern yourself about. A business associate, that's all."

"First I've heard of him."

"You don't hear about everything I do, Janice."

"Are you up to something shady, Freddie Maddox?"

"Not that's it any of your business, but no, it's all legit and above board."

"I don't want to be involved in any more shady deals."

"You're not involved, Janice. It's got nothing to do with you. This is my game. This place makes a mint but it's too seasonal. To get seriously rich you need to be making money the year round."

"You make money, Freddie, but you don't live."

"No, Janice. It's you who's wasting your life. In that grotty little art shop. It'll never make real money."

"I make real friends."

"Out of a bunch of losers."

"And sell something worthwhile, like art."

"Food isn't worthwhile, then? Holidays aren't?"

"Not the way you go about it."

"Look, Janice, I can do without this hassle. Just take care of the kid, will you, and be grateful for the lifestyle I'm giving you."

"That kid has a name, Freddie. She's called Felicity, and she's your daughter. I don't think you know how to love anybody, not your wife, not your daughter, not even yourself."

"You'd have helped your daughter if you'd persuaded that old biddy to sell her hotel to me when I asked you to."

"Not to you, Freddie, she wouldn't. Not to you. Not in a million years."

"There's a bloody fortune to be made there. High class, that's what it should be. Class, black tie dinners, exclusive. If it has to be arty, get that Lucian Freud feller down from London for the odd weekend. And who's that other bloke? Hockney? That's how to sell beds and meals. Personally, I'd go for a better class of punter than those artistic types, but that's just me."

"I'm going to the island now, Freddie. For once in your life act like a father and take Fliss to school."

******

The big day turned out differently to what everybody had expected. Not least because Sgt Brown of the County police chose that morning to investigate the theft of six paintings, as reported the previous day by Margot. He – and therefore the inn – turned a local event into a national one: he – and the inn – was on the early evening news nationwide and on the inner pages of some of the national press the next day.

"Crime One, Art Nil," said Janice.

"What do they say about publicity?" said JJ. "There ain't no bad kind? I might even sell a picture or two."

Kate caught up with Porlock as he looked at photographs of Margot's grandfather and the first hotel (the clapboard one) which he'd built on the island in the 1890s, making it the focus of the painters' colony. Several prints were hung on the wall by the double doors: sepia tinted and shot on glass negatives. In one, Margot's grandfather stood next to an upright Victorian gent

57

with a salt and pepper beard splayed out on his chest like a baby's bib – he was the man who, in his extreme old age, had painted the creamy chrysanthemums hanging a few feet away on the same wall.

It was a wonderfully compact gallery, full of such cross-references and follow-throughs. In the stern cabin, Janice's contemporary works tended to be figurative (of necessity: she had to sell them). There was still an art colony of sorts in the area and, as well as potteries, and two or three sculptors. A lot of painters had studios in the cheaper part of town among the chandlers, boat builders, sail makers, marine engineers, and shops selling beach umbrellas, sunglasses, flip-flops and buckets for sand castle building. Most of the workshops had sliding doors and backed on to a tidal creek. Each had its own slipway.

Because of the time span, you occasionally came across paintings where the easels had been set up in the same spot but a hundred years apart. Two, for example, were of the harbour, one from the summer of 1900, the other painted on the same spot in 2002. In the first, fishermen, true Victorians (born probably in the 1830s or '40s) smoked their pipes as the herring fleet was berthing. In the other, the harbour was merely a backdrop for holidaymakers with Anson's restaurant in the background.

JJ was the only artist whose works were hung in both the archive part of the gallery and in the stern cabin. His two paintings of the sand dunes – one with duckboards, the older one without – separated by a fifty years, hung however in the main body of the gallery.

After seeing everything on display, Kate and Porlock strolled in the hotel's grounds, ending up above the natural swimming pool in its own chasm-like cove. John Goldsmith was in the little boat down there rowing back from the sluice dam which let new water in and washed out the old. His daughter, a middle aged lady, stood waiting for him on pebble beach with folded arms.

"Shall we go down?" Kate suggested.

They climbed down the Jacob's Ladder brushing through the flowering plants and ivy which reached almost to the bottom. Campion he knew, and sea thrift, but what were these white stemmed flowers? Stalks white like the abele tree and with similar two-tone leaves: pale white undersides and dark green uppers? And were these dog daisies or scentless mayweed?

Once on the beach, they stood inside a drum of cliffs, enveloped by strangely coloured stone – a kind of coral or salmon pink. On one side, the cliffs were grooved vertically from top to bottom: across the pool they were striated horizontally with curious whitish bands an inch or so thick. Goldsmith made the dinghy fast to a ring bolted into the rock and he and Rebecca strolled over. "It's a mess," Goldsmith told them, "the dam needs a lot of work on it. The whole place does. Margot asked me to look into the possibility of a landing stage on the beach in the next cove along," he pointed to the west. "The one with the cave mouth. She'd be looking a million – minimum – for all the work that needs doing. In fact, you could spend that just making the cave secure and putting in proper stairs and stair hoists of some kind."

"One thing puzzles me," Porlock said. "If this place was once a haven for artists, how did the Montagues make ends meet? Most painters were never rich, after all."

"Toffs," Rebecca laughed. "The inn catered for the fast set with private money and sports cars."

"I suspect old Ma Montague charged them more," Goldsmith added, 'and either artists either less or nothing at all – many paid for their dinners with paintings."

"The ones in the vaults?" said Kate.

"Most likely."

"Do you think the burglars used the cave and tunnels to get away with the loot?" Porlock asked.

"Oh, without a doubt. The ladder I've been using has gone."

"How long was it there?"

"A month? I put it there when Margot first asked me to survey the caves."

"When did you last use it?"

"Ten days ago? Twelve."

"Nearer a fortnight," Rebecca put in.

"Have the police checked down there for clues?" Kate asked.

Rebecca looked at her. "I think that sergeant was just grandstanding. I can't see the county plod worrying too much about low value works of art."

"So there might be clues there?" said Porlock. "Can we get access."

Goldsmith, in turn, looked at Porlock. "Off the record," he said, "you'd be better off hiring a boat and landing on the beach outside the cave mouth. Even easy-going Margot wouldn't dare to let a guest loose in the caves. They really are dangerous."

"Who hires out boats?"

Rebecca gave them the name of a boat company in Brambletown.

"It'd be good to see the old place thriving again," Goldsmith said, as all four turned to walk across the beach to the foot of the wooden stairs. "I can just about remember in the pre-War days. We boys – and girls – were forbidden to come near the place. It was like Bohemia on Sea back then. Be a bit tame today, I dare say."

"You're a local boy?" Kate asked.

"Born and bred. Left to go into the Army during the War, of course, and then university. I never came back until I retired a few years ago. Went to the primary school in a village near here. It's an old folks' home now. That's one of the country's problems, isn't it? Not enough children, too many old codgers. What price the future without children?"

"We've done our bit," Rebecca argued. "Five children between us, and Lucy has one, and your grand-daughter Jenny will be having a baby soon."

"You should marry again, Becky," the old man said, repeated something he obviously said, forgetting the two strangers standing aside to let them climb the stairs first.

"Oh, Dad. Who'd want a fifty-four year old over weight widow with two grown up children?"

Porlock said: "A fifty-six year old widower who doesn't want to change nappies again?" All three looked at him: (Oh, God, he thought, bloomers and blunders again. All his life he'd blurted out things. This social intercourse thing wasn't easy. He blushed.)

CHAPTER 11

Next day, Kate and Porlock hired (chartered?) a big inflatable dinghy with an outboard motor and set out from one of the private quays off Fore Street. Gulls squealed and yelped and the painted town was bright in the sun. A foot ferry still crossed the river to an astonishingly yellow beach bordered by a forest which reached down to the shoreline. They passed astern of the ferry and headed on downstream to the Tudor fort which once guarded the hinterland. The ebb was with them until they reached open water.

"The tea-leaves must have come by sea," said Porlock as they cruised down at half throttle. "That means a small boat. Probably an inflatable dinghy, like this one, because it's easy to beach. Also easy to row. They'd have had to row, or paddle. Using an outboard would have been too risky. Sound carries a very long way over water, and everything would have been very still and quiet around three o'clock in the morning."

"Oh, come on now, Joss, even Sherlock Holmes couldn't be that precise."

"I bet he could. But there's another assumption here. I'm assuming they came out of Brambletown. They wouldn't have been able to row an inflatable against a four or five knot tide. They'd need the flood to get them there, and the ebb to get them back. Plus they'd need to do the whole thing in the dark and, given it's getting close to mid-summer when dark shrinks and light expands, we're talking about two or three o'clock in the morning. Put together the state of the tides, times of sunset and sunrise, take into account the weather forecasts and you could pinpoint the exact night the scrotes came and went."

"Scrotes? Joss, you're beginning to sound like one of that old police drama on TV – *The Sweeney*, wasn't it called?"

"*The Bill*, actually. It's where I learned to talk like a villain. Tea leaf is thief, half inch is pinch, as in steal."

"And any way," Kate ignored him, "everything you've said

is assumption. The painting could just as easily have been taken out to a ship."

"Of course, but this is a low value crime, isn't it? Meeting a ship at sea sounds expensive."

"We don't know that it is a low value crime." Kate argued. "We know the paintings wouldn't be worth much in Sotheby's but they might be of value to a private individual somewhere. Price is not the only reason why people value things."

"But it doesn't stack up any way you look at it, Kate. If you're talking ships, you're also talking a very wealthy individual. None of the stolen paintings is likely to be a masterpiece, so why not make Margot an offer she couldn't refuse? Twenty grand would've covered it."

"Because he knew Margot would never sell?"

"How would he know that?" Porlock asked.

"Or because an offer like that would arouse a lot of curiosity. He might not want questions asked."

"Or perhaps he's a local man who knows Margot and her little ways."

"Oh, I do hope not," said Kate. "That would be too awful. I'd rather believe the paintings were taken out to another boat, a bigger one?"

Porlock shook his head. "The Coast Guard look-out is just along the cliffs. They'd have been aware of a bigger ship, particularly one hove to at three o'clock in the morning. To the official mind that spells drugs and to the skipper of a boat that means interception on the high seas. And anyway," Porlock added, "a bigger vessel would have to put into a port somewhere and run the risk of the Customs and Excise rummaging about. Why not just land on a beach and be done with it?"

By ten o'clock they'd cleared the harbour and were steering eastward into the sun. Kelp swayed below the keel until they sailed into deeper water The sea was flat and of a perfect green except where it glinted in the morning light. Kate sat amidships in tight fitting clothes and a sun hat, which suited her, framing her face.

A long line of cumulus clouds rose high in the sky deep over the land: the coast, the sea and the island were in a cloud-free zone. The sun began to beat down. "And another thing, Miss

Holmes," Porlock remembered, "since you're solving all our problems these days, here's another one. We're assuming the burglar went after a specific picture. How could he be sure of finding it? Even Margot didn't know where things were down there."

"A guest? Somebody who booked into the hotel legitimately and so was free to prowl around in the small hours."

"Casing the joint?"

"Yes."

"A licence to prowl?"

"And not many doors seem to be locked in the inn, are they?"

"Easily pickable too, I imagine. No night porter, either."

"Once the guest had found the picture he wanted all he had to do was pick a few more at random and then hide them away in a place known only to himself and the man (or woman) who came for them in a boat. *If* that was the way it was done."

"Must have," Porlock argued. "The car park's half a mile away on the mainland. Is it feasible he could have got six moderate sized canvases out that way?"

"If that's all true," said Kate, "we could narrow it down to guests who checked in and out around those dates. Male, able bodied, even agile."

"Slept a lot during the day," Porlock added. "Yes, well you're probably right, but that's a job for the police. He may have been nothing more than the hired help. Mr Big's the guy we need to trace. And to do that, we'd need to know which of the six paintings was the one he wanted so badly. It all really does points to a local mastermind and the neighbourhood crook. The local drug runner, perhaps. There must be one."

Even at only four knots over the ground they were soon off the island. From the sea, in a fragile boat, the coast was mostly unapproachable. You couldn't land there and live. The exception was the cove with the cave, though it, too, was pretty forbidding, hemmed in as it was by dark cliffs which slipped into a blue sea. The rock leaned slightly backwards, too steep to climb but not too steep for brine-proof grass to get some kind of root-hold. Porlock ran the bow of their boat on to the beach, stepped ashore and drove the anchor into the sand. Kate handed him a hamper and then a large canvas bag with wooden rods for handles. "Change of clothes," she explained.

"Doubtful about my seamanship?"

"Doubtful about spray."

Then the accident happened. A ledge ran around the eastern corner of the cove. It was above high water and seemed to be a path to the bay around the bend. It was natural and ran only part of the way. Around the curve of the cliff, away from the small beach, the rock dropped sheer into quite deep water. While Porlock was making the boat more secure by tying the painter to a ring bolt he'd found in the eastern cliff, Kate strolled along the ledge, tripped, and fell into the sea. He heard her call, then the splash. He pulled off his shoes, clambered on the ledge, ran the five or six paces to where the sea was still boiling, and jumped in after her. At first there was a roaring in his ears and the seething whiteness of disturbed salt water. Kate had gone into the kelp. He saw her dimly and swam down and got his hands under her arms and locked them across her chest. He kicked upwards. Her lungs were still full of air and their buoyancy let him haul her up towards the bright sky. When they broke surface she began to splutter and panic. "Stop this," he ordered her very sharply. "*Stop it.*" She did. "All right," he then said more gently and quietly. "Put your head back on my shoulder so you can breathe." She did. He got them both up against the cliff and found something of a foothold to take a little of the strain off him for a moment. It was dangerous: they were below the high water mark and the rock was covered in barnacles sharp enough to cut flesh to the bone. "Just relax," he said as calmly and clearly as he could with his mouth slopping with sea water. "I promise you you'll float if you do. Everything's going to be all right. I'm carrying your weight at the moment but I can't for much longer. You must relax all your muscles. Just relax and you'll float. I promise you. I'm with you and I won't let you down."

"My hair'll go all frizzy," she wailed.

"I'll treat you to a perm."

"They don't have perms any more."

"Then I'll treat you to a hair cut and the barber can cut the frizzy bits off. Don't laugh. Why are you laughing? Kate. *Kate*, will you please stop laughing? For once in your life will you just do as you're told? That's better. Relax. Now we're going to lie on our backs. I'll be below you and I'll do all the swimming. Like a tug boat."

"I'm all right now."

"We have only a few feet to go. Trust me. I have a Life Saving Certificate."

"I'm all right."

"Okay, here we go." His elbows lifted her arms to the side and he pushed off from the cliff face. For a moment he thought they'd sink. Somehow she let go of her tenseness: her body became floppy enough for the sea to buoy her up. After two dozen strokes he felt sand below him. "We're in shoal water, now," he said, battling to catch his breath. "You can stand up."

"You've got your hands on my bosoms," she said.

He could scarcely breathe. They waded ashore and she turned either to hold him or, more likely, to be held. "Thank you," she said. "You saved my life."

"Well, I was getting a bit low on brownie points," he said as his breathing slowed and his heart stopped threatening to burst. "It was a quick way of topping up."

They collapsed and rested for a while. Kate was the first to sit up. She rummaged in her bag and brought out two towels. "Come on," she ordered him. "Get those wet clothes off and dry them on the rocks. You can use the towel like ... what are those things called – like skirts?"

" Loincloths? Kilts? "

"A kilt. Go and get changed by the cave. And don't look," she ordered him.

He walked up to the cave mouth. It was cold in there. There must be a Venturi effect, he thought, drawing air up through the tunnel to the top of the rock like a flue. The floor was sand and sea shells. There was a powerful scent of the sea. He stripped and dried himself. His torch was still in Kate's bag, but he went a little way up the steps, which were cut from the rock, without a hand rail, until the light dimmed too much to see by. He turned very gingerly, his legs wobbling with fatigue: and stepped down again carefully with a hand on the cave wall. He wrapped the towel around him and tucked it in. Outside the sunshine was hot and dazzling.

"You're a trained Life Guard, are you?" asked Kate. She'd changed into a long floral frock and was drying her hair.

"No."

"You said you were."

"I never did."

"I'm sure you did. And my hair's ruined. Look, it's all frizzy." She finished drying her hair and knelt down by the hamper.. "Are you dry? I don't want you catching cold."

"Kate?"

"Yes, Joss?"

"It's eighty in the shade. I'm more likely to get sunstroke than a cold. But, yes, thank you, I am dry And, no, I didn't say I was a Life Guard," he insisted. "I said I had a life saving certificate."

"Isn't it the same thing?"

"I got it," he confessed, picking up the torch, "when I was ten years old. In the local baths. I also had a certificate for swimming two lengths."

"And deceitful with it," she said. "I'm learning more about you all the time." And then: "Be careful," she called as he went back to the cave. He switched on the torch as he walked passed the steps deeper into the rock. It was floored with sand all the way. At the back the sand was dry: high water never reached too far in, apparently. There were one of two side-caves which suggested it might once have been an adit mine. Copper? Tin? Would mining have been worthwhile? Easy to ship out in small quantities, he supposed, though the coast must be wild in bad weather. There was, also, the ruin of an old jetty on the beach but which, he suspected, dated from the 1920s and '30s, the inn's great painting heyday.

The tunnel sloped upwards quite steeply, cutting across the western end of the island. Cautiously he began climbing, keeping his hand on the surprisingly smooth stone, following the beam of the torch. The walls closed in until he was it a flue-like tube. It opened out into a wider space at the foot of a rock face. Torch light picked out a ledge fifteen or twenty feet higher and the remains of a flight of wooden stairs. Along the bottom of the wall lay the missing ladder. It was one of those sliding metal ones. With an effort, he extended it, propped it against the ledge and climbed up. At the top he found himself on another flat space which again ended in a rock face, thought not so high. On the top of that, he could see the door which opened, he assumed, in the garden outside Palm Court.

To the right, however, a heavy door opened straight from the platform, presumably into the chambers below the inn. The door, which looked old, was very heavy, made up of thick slabs of timber held together by iron straps. The lock was big as well and, strangely, it had a thumb latch. Porlock went to press it down and then remembered finger prints – his, not the thief's. Gingerly, he picked up the hem of his towel-loincloth and tried it. The thumb latch clicked up and down but the inner latch was locked into the strike plate. He squinted into the key hole and the gap between lock and door jamb. Surely there was a faint glisten? He cocked his head to one side to get his nose close to the lock, and sniffed. WD-40? It had only been around for fifty years – younger than the iron lock and latch on the plank door. Fresh, too. How long would the smell linger? He shone his torch along the arc the door would describe when opened: but nothing. Only the oil suggested the door had been opened recently, in the last few days, probably. He climbed back down and walked along the tunnel to the beach.

Kate sat serenely by her picnic, quietly looking across the sea from underneath one of those fold-away umbrellas. It was brightly floral, throwing blue and red shadows across her face. "French bread and pâté," she explained. "Butter packed in ice. Tomatoes. Apple crumble and a little pot of cream in a flask to keep it cold. Camembert and Stilton. Followed, or preceded by, scones, clotted cream and strawberry jam. Take your pick. Or better than that, have a bit of everything. To drink we have elderberry cordial (very cold) and filtered coffee (very hot)."

"I'm going to write a play about you," Porlock joked. "It's going to be called *Kill Me, Kate*. No? All right, then what about *Cholesterol Kate*?"

"Did you see anything?" she asked, ignoring him. "In the cave, I mean."

He told her about the oil and the lock. "Otherwise a dead end," he concluded. "Disappointing. This is where we should find the vital but enigmatic clue. A half burned letter, a matchbook, a pen engraved with a strange name. But it's still quite an adventure. It reminded me of the time I climbed a mountain with a girl called Belinda."

"You've never mentioned her before?"

"That's because I haven't thought about it until now."

The shadow of the eastern cliff was half way across the cove when they decided to pack up and go. "Will you be all right?" he asked. "You're not afraid of the sea after what happened? I can drop you off on the other side of the island."

"No, thank you."

"You should wear a life jacket."

"It isn't very flattering for the figure."

CHAPTER 12

"Are you sure you want to come here, Kate?" Porlock asked her the following evening.

"Yes, Joss, I am. This is my thank you dinner."

"It's just …"

"You're thinking can I afford it, aren't you? Well, whether I can or not it's what I want to do. Though the place does look a bit …."

"Nautical? Or just plain naff?"

"As long we don't get sea sick."

They were in Anson's Restaurant, owned by Freddie Maddox. It was in the port's old sail loft and boat yard and themed as a 74-gun ship of the line circa 1790. There was a night club on the orlop deck. Dinner and lunch were served on the gun deck, the bar was on the quarterdeck. Dinner, by lantern light, was eaten at mess tables, secured to the floor but made to look as if they were slung on ropes from the deck head (or ceiling to landlubbers). Night clubbers drank by the light of purser's glims. Here and there, hauling on ropes or toiling at the guns, were waxwork models of Jolly Jack Tars.

They were having drinks on the quarterdeck and reading the menu. It was quite short. The Anson specialised in sea food for holidaymakers, its main customers. The management's boast – printed on the menu – was that everything they served was fresh: fresh from the farm or the sea that very day. Catering as it did for holidaymakers it also specialised in – and was famous for – its steaks and home-made garlic sausages.

"Whitebait!" said Porlock. "I haven't had whitebait for .. oh, thirty years? forty years?"

"Have some then, with brown bread and lemon. What about lobster thermidor?"

"Never tried it."

"What a lovely simple soul, you are, Joss."

"Thermidor? Wasn't that the Jacobins' name for August?"

"I don't know about that. I do know it's made with béchamel sauce and parmesan cheese. Egg yolks, nutmeg, cayenne pepper, tarragon, cream."

"Good Grief, Kill Me Katie, it sounds as fattening as whitebait."

"Let's go for it," said Kate. The waiter came over and they gave him their order.

"Do you know what Joyce in reception told me?" Porlock asked when he'd gone. "All the waxworks of the sailors in the restaurant have the same face – that of Freddie Maddox, the spiv who owns the joint."

"No!"

"So Joyce says."

"And he's married to Janice? Goodness, there's a mismatch there if ever I saw one."

The waiter came to take them to their table on the gun deck. The place was very nearly full of suntanned holidaymakers in casual clothes. As they passed by the tables they could hear the occasional "shiver my timbers" and "my hearties" and "Jim lad" as though Charles Laughton were still showing at the local Odeon. On the other hand, there were some nice prints of Rowlandson's naval characters on the tumblehome (or the bulbous sides of a ship as the glossary on each table explained.) Theirs was the Sea Cook, a man with a peg leg, a ladle, and a tankard of grog. He stood by one the great sea-going pots in which almost all the food eaten by a seaman in the sailing navy had been boiled. (Apart from ship's biscuit, that is, and the living weevils that came with it.)

"Good evening, folks. Is everything satisfactory?" It was Freddie Maddox, the owner, doing his rounds. Porlock looked at him: he seemed to be about forty-five but already running to seed. (Oil seed, Porlock thought unkindly.) He wore a scarlet cummerbund around a little paunch, a velvet jacket and a black bow tie. His forehead was broad and pale and his finger tips were splayed like one of those climbing frogs in those natural history documentaries you saw on TV. "Everything all right, folks?" he repeated.

"Fine, thank you," said Porlock.

"The whitebait's wonderful," Kate added, truthfully.

"Excellent. Excellent." He forgot them instantly as he spotted two men being escorted by the head waiter. "Gabriel! Gabriel Tomlinson as I live and breathe. And Gino. *Ciao*. Have I got something to show you both." Gabriel, who looked like a well-to-do middle-aged businessman, made a 'zip it' sign over his mouth. Then smiled and held out his hand. He said "*Ciao*", too. Gino, much younger than either of them, looked out of place: there was an air of innocence about him.

"What was that all about?" Kate asked when the trio were out of earshot.

"Dunno, but that Maddox boy is seriously weird." And then: "Where have we heard the name Tomlinson before?"

"*We* haven't," Kate said. "Not we because I haven't. Wasn't he an old time movie actor?"

"Not that one. Recently."

Kate swerved to another topic (something he soon learned was typical of her): "You seem to like paintings?"

"I know little about them except that some act like gateways to what seems like another place, some place beyond this world."

"You'll have to explain that."

"One day – when I understand it better myself."

She waited for him to say more. When he didn't, she went on: "Why don't you take up painting?"

"Little talent."

"Poetry?"

"Less talent."

"Music?"

"No talent."

"Novels?"

"Don't understand the human race."

"Photography?"

"Only if you don't need light meters and f-stops, whatever they are. Or Boots the Cash Chemist?"

Kate switched again. "You never talk about yourself," she said. "You're like a mystery man."

"No mystery. Nothing to talk about. That's all."

"What, nothing?"

"Yes. Nothing."

"Everybody has something."

"I don't. In fact, I've cut myself off from my personal past. Not the important past, just my own unimportant persoanl one. I'm not starting again. I'm starting out for the first time."

"You've cut yourself off completely?"

Porlock hesitated. "Almost. I've dumped a pile of books in storage."

"How many books?"

"About three thousand."

"That's a small library."

"Yes."

"Novels?"

"Some. Poetry and plays. Some philosophy, history, naval history, a bit of science, some politics. Art and a little theology."

"There's a kind of pattern to it, but a specialised one."

"It's an overview of the West and its evolution."

"That's what interests you?"

"Partly that. I've a better collection of books on Zen and Zen art than the London Library," he added.

"I'm getting to know a bit better. I know you're not married."

"How do you know that?"

"You told me."

"Did I? What for?"

"I asked you. On the harbour. The day we met."

"I see."

"Have you ever had a wife?"

"No, I haven't and, Kate, why am I being given the old third degree? I don't quiz you and you don't talk about yourself, either."

"I'm not very interesting."

"And neither am I."

"You told me about your name."

"That's about other people. What other people did. Not what I did or do."

"What about your father?"

"You don't give up, do you?"

"I want to get to know you."

"He was in the Army. Killed in Action. KIA. Okay?"

Kate paused for a moment. "I'm a widow. It wasn't a happy

marriage. In fact it was a bad one. I have a son in Australia. His wife doesn't like me so I don't see much off him. Two grandchildren. I had a job in the Civil Service. I have a pension and a three-bedroom flat in London. No mortgage. I looked after – nursed – my mother for ten years, two of them when she was bed-ridden. She'd died two months ago."

"Oh. It must have been hard."

"What they say about self-sacrifice is true. It can make you happy." She waited for him to say something more. When he didn't, she said: "What about that mountain?"

"Mountain?"

"You mentioned it yesterday. Belinda, wasn't her name?"

"Oh, that. That was a long time ago."

After the first course, he excused himself to go, as he said, to the heads which were, in fact, in what should have been the stern. He passed the table where Freddie was entertaining Tomlinson and Gino, the young Italian. Porlock found the door with the symbol of the little man with his legs apart. There was also a sign reading 'Jolly Jack Tars'. Yet think what you like about Freddie, Porlock thought, he does run a tight ship: the heads were spotless – not only clean but delicately perfumed. There was even a mural in tiles of a sea battle on the wall. (That whole coast was given over to art in one way or another.) Porlock washed his hands in liquid soap. On his way back he passed by the three men again.

"Kate," he said in high excitement when he got back to their table. "The damnedest thing's just happened. You'll never guess."

"Then tell me, if I'll never guess."

"I've just overheard a snatch of an Italian lesson. Do you know what *Gideon's God* is in Italian?"

"*Il dio di Gideone*?"

"Too right. They were talking about it at Freddie's table. Talk about loose lips sinking ships."

"It is strange, isn't it?"

"More than strange, Kate, it's downright weird. Or uncanny. Should we mention it to Margot?"

"Oh, I don't know, Joss," said Kate doubtfully. "No. No," she repeated with finality. "She and Janice seem to be very close friends. She might not like you talking about her friend's husband like that."

"Perhaps not. You're probably right. But Tomlinson? Tomlinson. Where have I heard that name before?"

"He was an old time movie actor."

"No. More recently than that. Very recently, in fact. No! Oh, well, it'll come back."

Lobster – and even the pudding – was a bit of an anti-climax after that but, not wanting to seem ungrateful, Porlock politely tried his best to please. All the same, both were glad to get out the restaurant and take a taxi back to the place which, to Porlock, already felt like home. A big moon followed them all the way and the tide was far enough out for them to walk the half mile to the island. Then they walked together to the stubby corridor which they shared. He turned to say good night to Kate.

"Don't lock your door for a moment, Joss, will you?" she said.

"Not lock it?"

"I have something for you. Just let me get it from my room. I won't be a more than a minute."

"Really, Kate, I don't need a present."

"See what it is first." She turned and left him. He'd washed his hands and face and even cleaned his teeth by the time she came back and knocked lightly on his door.

He opened it and she stepped in. She wore a long red silk dressing gown. He closed the door, draped the towel over its rail and stood back, hands on hips in his characteristic way. She slipped the gown off her shoulders, slowly, until both breasts were uncovered. He watched her. The gown dropped. She held out a hand to him. "Shall I draw the curtains?" she asked.

"No. The moon is shining very brightly."

CHAPTER 13

Porlock woke at three o'clock, vaguely conscious of something important. What was it? Then it came to him: where he'd heard the name Tomlinson – Joyce had been complaining about him, or his company, only a day or so ago. He was a wine merchant. But how did that fit in with Gideon? Perhaps there was a clue on the Tomlinson company website, if it had one, and it probably did. The inn had no computers for use by guests though wi-fi was available (was that the right word?). They could hardly ask to use the inn's computers because the damned things remembered every single place you visited. They might was well ask Margot outright about Tomlinson (and risk hurting Janice) as use her computer. Porlock rolled over: an internet café was the only way, and that meant another trip into town.

He told Kate over breakfast (tolerantly, she remarked how unromantic he was being) and they agreed to take the bus.

After breakfast, he waited for her on the rise above the mooring or parking space for the sea tractor. Art was everywhere, he reflected: even the ancient Cedar of Lebanon under which he stood had been shaped by the wind into a sculpture, streaming west to east in layers of straining branches. To the east the sun was spread blindingly all over the sea, broken only into silver waves with narrow black outlines, rolling back to uncover the sand of the isthmus. Bladderwrack of the darkest green and yellow were already exposed on the rocks where the tractor docked (or parked?). Soft waves ended in a sploosh and whoosh of spent sea.

On the other side, they walked around the headland to the village to catch the bus. The bright hot weather held. How long ago had the taxi brought him along these lanes? The bus called in at another village by the sea, as well as an inland one in a deep, steep-sided combe, and it was a good hour before they disembarked in town.

"How can we find a internet place?" Porlock asked as they stood once more in Fore Street. Kate pointed to a large policeman, the front of whose helmet was completely covered by the big silver badge of the county Force. He was also standing, incongruously, next to a public fountain attached to which was a notice forbidding the washing of fish in its water. The policeman pointed out the way to the café down one of the alleys leading to the river.

A dozen or so computers were ranged on a shelf around an otherwise bare room. Only two other people were there and Kate and Porlock were able to commandeer two swivelling office chairs. Google found the Tomlinson website in point one four of a second. As the home page flashed on the screen, they found themselves looking into the face of the Gabriel Tomlinson they'd seen last night in Anson's. He was a good-looking, in his fifties probably – but, as Kate remarked, there was something untrustworthy about him. More curious was the company's logo – a high, single span, bridge, so high it must cross a gorge. Or was it an aqueduct? The company had a London office though its headquarters was in a village in Tuscany.

"Odd to have an English wine company in Italy," suggested Porlock. "How do they cope with the local Godfather? Or his Godson?"

"It is a bit strange. It says the company was set up by Gabriel's father. If he's still alive he must be in his seventies or even eighties and retired. You're right, Joss, how did he come to set up business in an Italian village?"

"We could email for information." Porlock said. "Except it might give the game away."

"What game? We don't know if there is a connection between Gideon's painting and this man Tomlinson."

"Is it just a coincidence, do you think, that three things came together in one evening? Tomlinson, Jolly Jack Maddox, the painting – and Gino: four, if you count Gino."

"I can see why Tomlinson's has been pestering Margot," Kate continued, still reading the screen. "They're not at all big in this part of the country. They supply Anson's, as you'd expect. Probably that's how they met."

"Young Maddox is a bit of a Cockney wide boy or spiv (forgive the out-dated slang) and perhaps they met in London. Or the Smoke, as we villains used to say."

"There is this place which won some kind of award. *The Crown and Anchor*," Kate went on, ignoring him. "Not far from here."

"Shall we go there for lunch?"

"What for?"

"'To seek, to find and not to yield?' Any way it might be nice."

And so it was. A taxi dropped them on top of a surprisingly narrow headland where the ground dropped sharply away to a wide bay. The hillside leading down to it was wooded to the shore: below them they could see slender hazels, oaks (too twisted ever to have been worth felling), ash and chestnut. The bay itself was a narrow inlet, a tidal estuary. At that moment it looked more like a lake. Boats lay on their beam ends. Not in water, obviously – on mud, since the tide was out, but making. The opposite shore was timbered all the way to the top.

"My God," Porlock called suddenly, "look at this,"

"Look at what?" Kate was a few paces behind looking at patches of flowers: trefoil, ox-eye daisies and even a green-winged orchid. (Kate, he was to learn, had a passion for flowers – cut or growing in a garden rather than wild ones, but a flower is a flower.)

"This. Astonishing. Come and look."

"At what?"

"This."

"What is it?"

"Amazing."

"Yes, but what's amazing?"

"A steeple."

"A steeple?"

"A church steeple. It's almost touching the hill." Kate joined him in looking at the moss on the slates of a spire at eye level only ten yards or so away, in dense woods. It even had a weather vane though it must have been useless. "Why a weather vane?" Porlock wondered. "The only wind you'd get here is like that one in Westmorland – the Helm? You know, a down-draught off the hill. I bet it's rusted to its axle." But by then Kate was making her way down the hill through the woods. The spire, they discovered as they climbed lower, stood on a tower. What would the noise of the bells be like when they rang the changes?

The church itself almost filled all the flat land on the shore, forcing its grave yard to curve tightly around it. The door in the porch was locked. The village, if it could be called that, was across a creek on the next patch of flat ground: two or three cottages, a Georgian house, a chandler, and a pub. At high water boats could be launched down a slipway on cradles towed by cars. Now the tide was out and the place deserted. The Crown and Anchor (it had been a Royalist coast) turned out to be a Queen Anne house, now a small hotel catering for yachting people. They went inside.

"Business is a bit slack, is it?" Porlock indicated the empty bar.

"Slack water, slack trade, darling," the landlady smiled; an old joke, judging by the way she said it. "Slack water at low tide, that is. Things will pick once the tide turns. We'll be very busy this evening." She was a rather strapping woman, tall on high heels, big chested and heavily made up.

While this was going on, Kate had been reading the wine list. "You do seem to specialise in Italian wine," she said, looking up.

"Not just Italian," the landlady answered rather proudly, "Tuscan."

"Do you know Mr Tomlinson?" Kate asked her.

The landlady looked surprised. "We get our wines from his company," she said. "Do you know him, then?"

"*Of* him," said Kate choosing her words carefully. "Only of him. They say he's an expert on Italian wine."

"Well, yes, he's an expert all right, I will say that. But it was his father who started the business. I don't know the whole story but old Major Tomlinson was in Italy during the war. Don't ask me how or why."

"Is this their company?" Kate pointed to an address at the bottom of the wine list.

"*Tuscan Vineyards and Wineries*," said the landlady, leaning over to see. "Yes, that's them. They have an office and a winery in a village in the hills not too far from Lucca. Have you ever been there?"

"No,"Kate admitted. Porlock shook his head.

"Beautiful place. Wonderful. Such a beautiful place. We go there every two or three years, if we can. They mix tavola wines, mainly."

"*Tavola*?" Porlock asked.

"Table wines." The landlady turned to him. "What we call carafe or house wines. They sell Super-Tuscans, too, but not on the same scale."

Kate tried some of Tomlinson's table wine. "Good," she said, "though I'm no great judge."

Porlock picked up the bottle and read the label. "This bridge logo," he said, "it's a bit unusual, isn't it? Does it signify anything? Mean anything?"

"That I don't know, darling."

"It's not a bridge near the winery?"

"Oh, no, I do know that."

"A Roman connection perhaps?"

"That I don't know either, sweetheart. Major Tomlinson would know, of course – he must have chosen it."

After the landlady had gone Kate said; "What did she mean – Major Tomlinson was in Italy during the War?"

"Dunno," said Porlock. "The whole 8th Army was, not to mention the Americans."

"And where do we go from here?"

"On a jaunt to Tuscany."

"Whatever for? We have no real reason for doing that."

"We have. Remember Tennyson's *Ulysses*: "To strive, to seek, to find, and not to yield.' The Gulfs might wash us down or we might meet the great Achilles in the Happy Isles." Porlock hesitated and looked out of the window at the boats keeled over in the mud.

Kate said: "What is it?"

"I was just wondering ...."

"Yes?"

"Well ... I was just wondering if there's a laundrette in town. Or if the inn does laundry. I need to wash some shirts. And socks."

Kate was visibly holding back her laughter. "Who are you

going to meet?" she burst out. "The great Achilles?"

"Even Ulysses had to change his socks," said the crestfallen Porlock.

Kate could hold back no longer and laughed peal after peal of laughter. "Oh, Mr Porlock, what am I going to do with you?" she managed to get out a good two minutes later when the laughter eased off, only to break out again. "Oh! Oh," she said at last, "Oh, I do love you, Mr Porlock."

CHAPTER 14

Before they left for Italy (the inn did do laundry), Porlock bought a digital camera. Why, he wasn't quite sure (he'd never taken a photograph in his life) but thought vaguely it might be useful for recording evidence, or something. That evening he tried his hand at landscapes and seascapes and rather liked what he'd done. In fact, he was – in his own words – 'smitten'. Next he tried portraits – mainly of JJ and Margot, both of whom were always helpful when it came to art, even a doubtful art such as photography. Finally, he tested himself on the pictures hanging in the new gallery, particularly the dancing couple and the painting of Margot in her youth. Not bad.

Early next morning, JJ gave them a lift to the spinal road which ran through the county and dropped them outside the Red Lion in a village just off the highway. It was the pick-up point for the coach which stopped at Heathrow on its way to Victoria bus station in London.

At take-off, the flight to Pisa was full: Kate and Porlock got the last two seats, next to each other but on opposite sides of the aisle. For the first hour, Porlock read the instruction manual which came with his new digital camera. 'Idiot-proof' the woman in the shop had said: but, then, she'd never met anybody as technically idiotic as Porlock. In the end, he settled for 'auto-mode'.

He leaned across the aisle. "Given the rate of change, I reckon that by 2010 cameras will be operated by thought alone. Point and Think. Or perhaps they'll tell you what they're going to shoot, and then do it." She looked at him but said nothing and turned back to her book. For the first half hour, Kate, who knew a little Italian ("evening classes one winter"), mugged up a bit more. For the second half, she read an Aurelio Zen detective novel.

"Is that the one where Zen ends up in Iceland with the trolls?"

"No."

"Fairies?"

"No."

"Wycliffe's better. All those decaying Cornish mansions and centuries old families on their last genetic legs. Feeble head of the house, gaunt and bitter sister-stroke-aunt, sensitive son, enigmatic daughter." Kate went on reading. "Wycliffe got better as he got older. So does P D James. Funny, isn't it, we never see the poetry Adam Dalgleish is supposed to write yet Miss James is writing near poetry in her own late prose. On every page who find first syllable rhymes like 'random, rancid, rankle, ransom'. And she's getting on bit. There's hope for us all, isn't there. Kate? Kate? Kate?"

" You're full of surprises, Joss. I thought you'd be more a fan of Plato than detective novels." She put her book down and looked at him for a while. "But," she said at last, "you haven't lived all your life in books, I do know that. Belinda," she said. "Tell me about Belinda and the mountain. That was something you did, not just read about."

"It's a long story."

She looked at her watch. "We have a full hour before we land."

All the same it was another ten minutes before he was cajoled into talking about it.

******

"Would you like to see some cave paintings?" a young woman had asked him one Saturday evening at a barbecue in somebody's garden. It was the first time they'd met.

Were cave paintings the same as etchings? he wondered. But: "Where?" was what he said. "Spain?"

"Fool! We have our own home-grown ones about a hundred miles from here. Corrugated roads but an easy drive. The climb up the mountain's the hard bit. One day up, one day down."

"You're going in a party?"

"No. Just the two of us."

Porlock stared at her, a very tanned faun-like young woman with small breasts, long legs, long hair and a very white-toothed smile. "The two of us?" he repeated. "Just you and me? Alone?"

"Huh-huh."

"When?"

"Next weekend?"

"Well, at least I'm free then."

"Where are you staying?" He told her. "I'm Belinda, by the way," she'd said over her shoulder as she left. "Be ready to go by seven o'clock. In the morning."

Was it a hoax? he'd wondered all that week but she did turn up – abruptly, in a noise of car: a Deux Chevaux. "I love these cars," she told him. "They're so funny and so very French."

"Made by a local blacksmith out of corrugated iron sheeting by the looks of it," Porlock said. "Like a bit of a Nissen hut."

Surprisingly, she drove carefully. Even so, by mid-day they were parked in the middle of a pass between two ranges of hills. They ate a picnic lunch from real crockery plates which Belinda had made, painted, glazed and fired herself ("I'm no potter. Tried it for a bit, that's all.") and then got ready for the long hike on foot. At first the valley was narrow and scattered with rocks like resting sheep. The hills on either side held the air still and hot. At first, too, there was a rough path, then only the stream to guide them, and thickets of sharp trees if they strayed. Skin was already sore with sun and sweat. Soon the valley broadened and they were in the mountains proper. "That's where we're going," Belinda said, pointing to a distant peak, clear and sharp against the afternoon sky.

By late afternoon they'd reached a pool in the river with flat land on one side, a cliff on the other. "Camp ground," Belinda said, slipping out of her rucksack. They piled twigs together to light a fire and Porlock was sent foraging for small logs. Supper was steak and baked potatoes and tea made in a billy can with brown river water. With the short twilight came the grating screech of insects, rising and falling in pitch. With the night came the cold. The backs of their hands burned with it.

"The people who made the paintings must have known this place," Belinda said, speaking over the rim of an enamelled mug of tea. "Can't you sense them?"

"All I sense is the cold."

"They must have been tiny people and delicately made."

"But tough, surely. You can't sentimentalise them."

"I think they lived half in this world and half in an eternal one. My belief, though maybe nobody else's. The light up there is terrific, perfect," she went on. "I love the thought of those paintings just being there in that amazing light while whole civilisations rose and fell all over the place. It's the ultimate in stillness, although the paintings are really captured motion"

"*E*-motion, did you say?"

"Motion. And emotion. They are so full of energy there's stillness in their non-stillness if you see what I mean."

"Not really."

"You'll see for yourself tomorrow when we get there."

She stoked the fire with fresh logs. Stars vibrated in a midnight-blue sky. The Southern Cross, from Porlock's northern point of view, replaced the Plough and Pole Star. Then the moon came up over the mountains. There's a rabbit in the moon south of the equator. To a northerner everything's upside down. The valley filled with moonlight. It gleamed on the rushing river and brought on a very cold night. Chill seeped up through the sleeping bags.

In the morning Belinda was up first, re-kindling the fire and making coffee in the billy-can he'd bought. She gave him a breakfast of canned grapefruit and bacon, then handed him the rations for the day's march. They looked liked boot-laces. "Biltong," she explained. "Dried buck venison." Porlock filled four ex-Army water bottles in the brown, bilharzia-free river, and threaded them on his belt. Biltong and oranges he stowed in a small rucksack. They took only what they needed; the rest would be there when they got back that evening. Then they set off in the morning coolness. Both shivered a little till they reached the first real slopes and began to climb sharply into the woods, hauling themselves up by tree trunks, snatching at handfuls of dust still cold with the night.

Respite came, for a short while, only when they were able to walk along a contour among more slender trees, little bigger than saplings, with dry, hard, shiny leaves. Then they climbed again. A little higher up, trees gave way to spiky, crabbed shrubs and then they were above the tree-line in the full glare of the sun. The early, spotlessly white, mist had boiled off the peak. Now the sky itself was white with the peak grey against it. Dry air scorched their open, panting, mouths. Below the peak the land was grey-green with stone. Climbing now they felt the strain in their thighs and nearly bursting hearts. Once or twice Porlock almost blacked out and when his sight slowly came back he was looking through a deep yellow haze. His head rang and his chest was dry and aching. Water in the bottles was almost hot. They rested in the shadow of a rock.

"Want to go back?"

"Yes," said Porlock truthfully.

"You'll do."

It was cool in the cave. If a cave it really was, and not just a very deep overhang. And there they were, the paintings, in the inner part where the darkness was more like soft light. "Look up," Belinda told him. "Elephants." Painted ochre elephants on living rock, so perfect, so impressionistic, so right, and made with so few brush strokes. Where had the painter learned his art? "Astonishing," Porlock said. "So simply drawn. So lifelike."

"Better than lifelike. It's another life in itself."

"New life forms? Do you really think so?"

"Yes, I do. They've been given a kind of life, if only in our minds. And a certain immortality, too. What are our seventy years to their seven hundred, seven thousand, seventy thousand?"

"And gazelles?"

"Springbok. Perfectly observed. See them leap?"

"Oh," said Porlock, "and men." Hunters with long spears and swollen buttocks.

"Hunters and painters," Belinda corrected him. "And women. And birds."

"Where?"

"There, above your head."

"I can't see anything."

"Just keep looking at those marks." The marks were simple brush strokes, as if the artist had just been testing whatever he (she?) used for a brush. Then, suddenly, the lines became a flock of birds in flight.

"And here," Belinda said. "Look at this."

"A hand print? A real one?"

"Yes. I'm told you can make out the fingerprints with a

85

magnifying glass." The painter must have had his hand smeared all over with reddish ochre and left the imprint on the roof of the cave where he'd flattened his palm to steady himself. It was as small as a modern child's. How did such a small man reach there? The roof was too high for Porlock to touch with the tips of his fingers even when he jumped.

"Piles of stones, perhaps?" Belinda put in, reading his mind.

Not wanting to speak, he went and sat on a rock outside the cave for a while. There was more sunlight to the square inch here, he thought, than anywhere else on the planet. Heat and air touched him a like soft cloth. He looked over the dead silent valley, empty except for sunlight, and felt the painter's eyes gazing at him from among the boulders over there. No. No, that was wrong. Over there was only the lidless eyes of a mountain viper or adder, stumpy and venomous. The man lived in paint on the living rock and looked at him not through light and space but time. He got up to look at the paintings again.

"You are moved, aren't you?"

"Yes," Porlock said.

"It's my private Sistine Chapel."

******

"That was my Hemingway away-day," Porlock finished. "I never saw her again. She'll be an old woman now, if she's still alive."

CHAPTER 15

They had breakfast in the garden of their hotel, an ex-tobacco factory, in the suburbs north of the city's walls. "Reality can't match imagination,"Porlock remarked. He was reading a brochure about Elba. "I mean, reality can't match mental images. Listen to this ... 'the romance of the seas around Elba, littered as they are with wrecks, wine jars, and antique wine.' Wrecks and antique wine. Beautiful, isn't it? Good enough to transport you to the Great Elsewhere. But if you could physically sniff the stuff would it be half as good as that? In other words, are images inside the mind stronger than reality outside it?"

"Do you want more toast with that honey?"

"No. No, thank you."

"You don't eat enough, Joss."

"Kate, I've been catering myself, all on my own, for the best part of half a century. The fact that I'm still here suggests I've been eating .... well, at the very least, *enough*."

"You should still eat more, all the same. You're a man, after all."

"Not a very big one. Thank God. I'd hate to be big and gross. Think of all that methane. On second thoughts, don't. It doesn't bear thinking about."

"You'll have more coffee, I suppose?"

"Yes. Yes, please."

"When we get back I'm going to buy you some tooth whitening toothpaste. The way you drink coffee you'll have black teeth."

"It's a substitute for alcohol."

"It isn't good for you."

"Listen to this: '*Elba Rosso*,'" he read aloud, "has a winey nose. *Winey* nose. Lovely, isn't it? Or what about this .... 'a wine as red as a ruby mellowing to amber in the bottle – a wine whose bouquet is of roses, cherries, and the brushwood of a wild forest'. Good, isn't it?"

"Joshua, you don't take a blind bit of notice of anything I say, do you? It's as though we've been married for forty years, and yet we've only just *met*. What will you be like in ten years time?"

"Ten *years*? Good Grief, madam, I don't intend to be alive in ten years. And, besides, I do listen."

"Well, I'm not listening to you, not when you talk like that. You will be here in ten years' time and that's that. I'm going upstairs to get ready. Are you ready?"

"Oh, yes."

'*Elba Rosso* has a winey nose', he read again. Wonderful, he thought. Wonderful (but what does it mean?). Something, in any case, to store in the mind along with the fact that chestnuts were once the staple of the mountain people of Elba, or October's re-colouring of the island. (Was the PR man who wrote this stuff a poet?) The chances were Porlock would never go to Elba, but did it matter? With this brochure you could get there while sitting in a coffee shop in the Tottenham Court Road where the girls have barbed wire tattooed around their ankles. On the other hand, in translation *Elba Rosso* read differently. *Red Elba*'s winey nose brought W C Field to mind – either him or a hard-drinking, left-wing, feminist blogger in dungarees with half the bib hanging down. Elba, he noticed, is also lobster-shaped. Odd that.

Kate came back, dressed for going out. (Even Porlock could see she had a good dress sense when she put her mind to it – which seemed to do every day now.) "Ready?"

He left the brochure on the table. "I left Elba on the table," he said when they were near the door. "Elba table. There's a sort of palindrome in there, isn't there?"

"You're a lovely man, Joshua. But, Goodness me, you are weird at times. What *am* I going to do with you?"

The early morning freshness was already lifting as they walked along streets lined with hot weather architecture: yellow or ochre stucco, thick red Tuscan tiles, balconies shaded by eaves, awnings, dark green shutters, and trees. The trees, lining the pavements and filling the gardens, were a surprise to Porlock: he'd expected maquis or perhaps thorn scrub. The city was on a plain ringed by green mountains. What looked like pale white peaks beyond them were, it turned out, marble quarries.

The city walls astonished him, unbroken as they were, and lined in a complete circuit with ilex and chestnut trees. A two-lane road ran around the top in a complete loop. A stream flowed under the wall. Barracks and parade grounds (what kind of arms drill?) were once hidden in the great heart-shaped bastions. Early morning joggers trotted in what shade they could find: dog walkers took the sun. Walls and bastions were made up of uncountable millions of red bricks almost as thin as tiles. "Look," he said, "look. Doesn't it remind you of Rye?"

"No."

"No? All those hand-sized medieval bricks?"

"No, because I've never been there."

They passed into the city through St Mary's Gate, with its great iron studded door and painted low-reliefs of the Virgin and Child, into a triangular square with traffic swirling by on either side. Facing them was a greengrocer, a bicycle hire shop and a map of the city on a pole. Distinctly, it showed the rigid grid of the Roman town intercut by mazes of medieval streets in a perfect example of the art of compaction, everything packed away like veins, arteries and organs in a body. The amphitheatre was obviously outside the Roman walls but very much within the Medieval and Renaissance ones.

After an hour or so they stopped for coffee in a *caffe* in a miniature square. "You take an interest in all kinds of odd things from odd angles, Kate remarked, "and no interest in what most people take an interest in."

"An alien, you see. My ambition in old age is to be an alien at ease."

"When does old age begin?"

"In five years."

"Only five?"

"Old old age will come along in ten. I won't be here for that. Not according to the Master Plan."

"What does that mean?"

"It means I'm never going to be an octogenarian, not if I have any say in the matter."

"And what will happen to me? Have you thought of that?"

"Well, no, to be honest. You're five years younger than me."

But Kate wasn't listening: she walked ahead of him, pointedly. Freed of the need to talk, Porlock looked around more intently. Mostly it was a beige or yellow city with dark green closed window shutters (was the colour municipally decreed?). All the houses, without exception were five or six storeys high yet opening on to streets perhaps only five or six yards wide. It was an intensely urban and canyon-like city: nothing of nature was here, only people and human thought.

Yet five or six cities were also packed away in that half square mile: an amphitheatre, a Napoleonic end, a 19th century opera house and *albergo*, the river (unromantically called 'the ditch'), palaces and churches. The priests and the dukes had gone. A few well-used fashionable thoroughfares were packed with people solidly filling the lanes from side to sidewalk-less side. Cyclists somehow got tolerantly through without the use of bells.

And then there were the empty quarters and silent lanes. These appealed to Porlock the most: voices in mazes, voices in empty streets, a glimpse (perhaps only a hint) of mysterious figures disappearing barely seen around corners. Standing alone in the lanes you could be in any century out of the last eight, until a cyclist rode silently by: What are they doing? Thinking? Why were they living here in this a strange place, a city of priestless churches and dukeless palaces? You stepped from blinding sunlight into shade but brought the sun with as an afterglow in your eyes. Sunlight brought out the beige of the painted walls, but also darkened it in the shade, or threw oblique shadows of the tile-like bricks where they were exposed by the fall of stucco.

What interested Porlock about the palaces were their hiddenness: their massive wooden doors with antique brass bell-pulls recessed in brass niches and cave-like passageways leading to wrought iron gates opening into the courtyards and gardens with palms and orange trees. Everything was natural with decay and disrepair.

Were these churches designed for bright sun light and strong shadows? Reflected sunlight from the marble of San Michele brought out the ancient redness of the tile-like bricks high on the houses behind it .The deep toned bell, so medieval sounding, tolled the quarter hours. Eleven o'clock. A town in time. Where were the hooded monks and begging friars? The leper bells? Porlock felt the encircled spirituality of the place, but also that it had become a museum of the spiritual.

Continuously, he took photographs of it all, and also of Kate's back as he strolled patiently on ahead. Sunlight, he quickly discovered, was vital. So much so that he had doubts about taking pictures back in England. Already he valued light, colour, shape and texture, all set off against a backdrop of blue sky.

Kate paid sixty cents to use the toilets in the Via Pescheria. She came back to find him crouched down measuring the cobbles with this thumb. She stood over him for a few seconds until he noticed her. Clearing his throat, he stood up and presented his bent right thumb to her. "The thumb," he explained, "is roughly one inch long from knuckle to nail. These cobbles are roughly three inches by three. Furthermore the street is only five yards wide."

"Yes?"

"The cobbles are also laid out in fan shapes."

"Yes?"

"So walking creates an optical illusion. The whole street appears to be in perpetual motion."

"You're so like a little boy at times."

"No, I'm not. I just take an interest in things."

They walked together down the crowded lanes. A big event – an exhibition of comics – was taking place in several marquees from St Michael's to Cathedral Square. The streets were jammed with young people in fancy dress – presumably copies of the costumes worn by their comic book heroes. Presumably, too, the comic book heroes were Italian: they recognised only Batman and Spiderman. (Where was Superman?)

By now they were in the yellow oval of the amphitheatre with its ragged skyline of different sized buildings. Many of the buildings, at street level, were *caffès* or *gelateria* each with its spread of tables in the open air. "Let's go over our options again," Porlock said. "Would you like to sit down?"

"No. Keep walking and talking."

"Well, we agree there are two approaches. First to broach Tomlinson via his winery. Secondly to try and find out who in all Italy is interested in Gideon."

"Tackling Tomlinson is risky. The Mafia might be involved."

"Capo and kaput, eh? Not likely though, is it? I can't see Freddie as a hit man. He's not exactly how you'd imagine Big Louis from Chicago."

"He might be a pawn. Being used."

"By the Godfathers? Freddie is strictly small time. That's my guess."

"All the same, we don't know."

"No, we don't"

The centre of the oval was given over to market stalls selling gold leafed icons, painted pottery, etched pebbles from the river (not the city's own stream but from the Serchio outside the wall), illuminable paintings, sweets, peg bags (*peg bag*s?), leather belts, *brigidino* which look like giant potato crisps. Porlock stopped at a stall selling hand-made boxes with marquetry Tuscan landscapes in shades of brown on their lids; hedgeless fields, a solitary poplar, a solitary farmhouse on the skyline.

"How do we find out who's interested in Gideon?"

"Advertise," said Kate. "In the local paper."

"The trouble is we could have done that from the island."

"Well, next stop has to be the town art gallery."

It had turned noon and the tables in the oval were nearly all full. They found an empty space next to a short palm tree in a terracotta tub. And in the afternoon they drew another blank: nobody in the city art world had ever heard of Gideon Comely. Their best bet, they were told, was to try smaller galleries in smaller towns. Private collection, by definition, would be officially unknowable. Even if anybody knew unofficially, they'd need the owner's permission to let the world know about it. (Was that true? Kate wondered.)

"Our memory's filling up fast," Porlock said, checking out the camera. "We need to find a camera shop. To strive, to seek, to find, and not to yield."

Next morning they went along to Verdi Square, close to the ramparts, to catch the bus to a mountain village with an art gallery. The drive took them away from an unspoilt town into spoilt countryside with dozens of factories winding along the banks of the river. The factories followed them even into the foothills of the high mountains. Then, suddenly, industry was left behind and they re-entered the Middle Ages.

The bus climbed high into the mountains and stopped at a narrow terminus below the town or village walls. Was it a village? If so, this was a village-sized-city with ramparts, a cathedral, and a medieval maze of streets (silent, sunlit or shaded) which turned suddenly into staircases or vanished mysteriously in a slide of cobbles around secret bends. It was also a city-village of solid five and six storey houses and palaces which could be easily used as the location for a movie of a Jacobean play about Renaissance revenge. Beige, yellow and ochre were the prevailing colours, either boosted by sunlight or darkened by shade. Porlock was already quick with the camera, zooming in or out and framing in an instant, seeing shots without seemingly looking.

And still those odd questions crowded into his mind. Was the narrowness of the alleyways for shade and coolness, or defence? To the west, at the ends of narrow lanes, were sudden vistas of the marble quarries on the high mountains stark against that astonishingly blue sky. The lower flanks of the mountains were forested but dotted with farms. In the city-village they encountered odd courtyards with mysterious rooms set high in otherwise unbroken walls. The sun was hot, the shade cool and yellow with reflected light. There were no cottages, but there were palaces, and a lot of ancient public art. It was also a city of steepness. "No city for old men," Porlock announced, watching two old men with sticks straining to walk. The bells of the cathedral tolled the quarter hours. 11.45 am.

The Public Gallery was part of an old palace. Above the gate was a painting of the Virgin and Child in a roundel surrounded by a frame of fruit and green leaves. The curator, if that is what she was, spoke no English, and the name Gideon Comely meant nothing to her. It was not that she knew little about him – she knew nothing at all, and seemed to doubt that anybody with such a name could amount to much, artistically.

A bit disconsolate, they went into a bar-cum-grocery store to eat. Kate's night school Italian got them bread, cheese, ham and salami on large squares of paper in place of plates. The cheese and bread were dry and hard. "Right for a city-village in the hills," was Porlock's verdict.

It was cool inside, with a red tiled floor, a wooden ceiling, and a dado of unadorned stone with whitewashed plaster above. Shelves of bottles – what they were they didn't know; Amara said one bottle, Amoro said its neighbour. Higher up were polished wooden shelves for boxes and biscuits, an accordion next to a mandolin next to a finely beaten copper vase of flowers. Paintings, recent and locally done, were of the duomo with poplars and a background of mountains.

"You can't get away from time in this country," Porlock said as he ate salami and hard, butterless bread. "Look at this strange old city on a mountain with the Carrera marble quarries on the skyline. Isn't it a pity that all time isn't present at the same time, if you know what I mean."

"No."

"No, it isn't a pity?"

"No, I don't know what you mean."

"Well, wouldn't it be wonderful if we could know everything that happened the day Mr Comely painted that picture. We wouldn't need to see it physically. We'd see in our minds and also know why he painted it. We'd know what depths there were in the man."

"You read too much into people," Kate said after a slight pause. "Most people are not that deep."

"Gideon was, I hope."

"I hope so too for your sake but depth isn't something most people want or understand."

"We can't accept the hegemony of the shallow, though, can we?"

"Yes, Joss, you can because you have to. There are billions of them and very few of you. The dominant personalities who run the world aren't deep. If anything they're extremely shallow. Nor do you usually become rich through thinking deep thoughts. You do so by selling something which masses of people want to buy and masses of people have no use for deep thoughts. You're a deep man," she concluded. "It's your nature but, Goodness me, you do need looking after."

"I get by."

"Then what's all this seeking and not yielding all about? Most men of your age would be putting their slippered feet up and grumbling about mowing the lawn."

"That's unkind. I don't deserve that."

Kate looked at him. "No," she said almost with tears in her eyes. "You don't deserve that. I"m so sorry."

"That's all right. What you say is true."

It was time to go back when the new memory was nearly full. They caught a blue Lazzi bus from the terminus opposite a sleazy looking bar and headed back to Lucca. Over dinner Kate said: "Tomorrow we're going to hire a car and drive up to the winery. We have to tackle this head on."

"Driving on the right?"

"I'll drive."

CHAPTER 16

The wine cellars were in a small castle-like building. To get a feel for they place, they joined a guided tour, for a fee, and followed a group of Americans down a long, gently sloping stone staircase. The wine barrels (vats? hogsheads?) were enormous – wooden, red rimmed, strapped with iron bands, each with a shiny metal spigot. The barrel ends were at least six feet high and of an oval shape. Dozens of them lay side by side, stretching away into the darkness at the end of the tunnel-like cellar. The cellar, in fact, reminded Porlock of London Underground's Bakerloo Line – it had once been a steam railway and one side of the stone vaulting of the cellar was blackened as though by smoke. Filled, unlabelled, bottles lay in the next underground chamber: rack after rack of them, lying on their sides and thick with dust. Next door – in the old castle dungeon or prison house – were ready-for-sale bottles wrapped in straw jackets.

It was all very interesting but getting them nowhere. A tunnel led under the road to what at one time must have been an old – and very big – barn but where you could then buy bottles of wine, books and DVDs, maps of Chianti (one of which Porlock bought) and trivial mementoes like key rings with the Old Bridge logo. The company offices were there also, around the side, with a reception desk and a rather good-looking receptionist.

Inevitably, there was also a catering area with outside tables and a view of the Chianti hills to the east. They were heading for this *caffè* to talk things over when Kate suddenly said: "Don't look now."

"Don't look where?"

"Behind you."

"I had no intention of doing so until you mentioned it."

"Let's get around the corner."

"Kate, what is it?"

"I'm not sure. All right, stop here. Look around the corner but don't make it obvious."

Cautiously Porlock did as he was told. He saw nothing out of the ordinary – just tourists milling about in a winery. "What am I supposed to be looking at?"

"That tubby man over there"

"What tubby man?"

"In the Panama hat."

"What's a Panama hat?"

"Oh, Joss, don't be so annoying. The straw hat with the ridge on top."

Porlock peered around the corner again: "No! It's not Jolly Jack himself, is it?"

"I thought so. Is it? I think so."

"I'm pretty certain it is. Oily as ever even without the cummerbund. What's he up to in the middle of the holiday season?"

"And isn't that the young man we saw in Anson's with Tomlinson?"

"Gino? Could be. We only saw him for a few minutes, though. Could be, all the same. What are they talking about, I wonder."

"Something important, obviously." What was the looked on Gino's face: sheepishness? Sulkiness? Distress?

"What shall we do?" Porlock wanted to know.

"Follow Maddox."

"Follow? As in tail? Kate, we're not undercover cops in downtown LA."

"He doesn't know us. He never even glanced at us that evening in Anson's. We can follow him safely without him suspecting anything."

"We'll be talking about Mickey Finns next. And cute broads and plug-uglies with saps." By now they were in the car park in the full blaze of the Tuscan sun. Freddie Maddox got into the driving seat of a black Mercedes People Carrier with GB plates. "He drove here," Porlock observed. "What was he carrying?"

"Get in the car, Joss," Kate ordered. She put on her sun glasses. "Quick as you like." She started the engine. Prematurely, as it happened. Maddox went back into the winery. He was there for a good ten minutes. Coming back they noticed he looked jumpy and nervous, though he was still

97

taking no precautions. He didn't look around at all.

This time Maddox started the engine and moved off slowly, tyres softly crunching on the gravel of the car park and driveway. At the main road, he turned left, heading west towards the coast. The sun was going down. Kate followed but instinctively chose the left side of the road. "Kate!"

"I know. Don't you think I know? Did he notice?"

"I don't know," Porlock, almost in shock, answered. "Not that it matters." He pulled down both sun visors. "The sun would have glared off the windscreen. He couldn't see in. And anyway we have local plates."

"I don't want to crash. It's stupid having to drive on the wrong side of the road like this."

"Well, please don't even think about driving on the right one."

"I don't want to lose him, either."

"I think he's turning off to the right."

"Sure?"

"No. Turn right at the next junction, though."

"What if you're wrong?"

"I'm pretty sure. But there are a good fifteen cars between us now and he's going fast."

Too fast for Kate. They lost Freddie before they reached the hair pin bends carrying the road down to a plain broken vertically only by poplar trees and a tower crane working on a small private house. They rounded another bend, now out of sight of the plain, and looked down on a gross looking bridge – cantilever was it called? Or truss? Whatever it was, a D-shape of girders carried it across the central span. The river was dizzily far below. Above them, on their right, was a campanile, probably belonging to a monastery. Above them, on their left, were the ramparts of the village-city they'd already visited. They turned right before reaching the bridge and then drove in a loop down under it. Maddox was nowhere in sight.

"What a nuisance," Kate fretted. "We almost had him. We nearly solved the whole mystery."

"Kate, can you pull over and let me get a shot of that viaduct back there."

"Joshua Porlock, I'll murder you. How can I stop on these

hairpin bends? With all this traffic?"

"In that case can you turn round at the bottom of the hill and drive back up again?"

"No, I can't. Take a picture over your shoulder. Or out of the window as we go round this bend. Oh, my God..."

Porlock did – took a picture as Kate almost locked the steering wheel to take a particularly sharp bend, so sharp it opened up the whole valley again. He pointed the camera in the general direction of the bridge and pressed the button: click, click, click. He pressed the view button. "It isn't the same bridge as the one on the bottle," he said, looking at the pictures on the monitor. "I wonder when it was built?"

"Ask Mr Goldsmith."

"Good idea. I'll e-mail Joyce and ask her to ask him."

"Joss, I was being sarcastic."

"Well, it's a good sarcastic idea."

They stopped off at their hotel to shower and change before going in the city for dinner (the hotel served only breakfast: no other meals). The middle aged man on Reception helped Porlock upload the photographs of the bridge and showed him how to send them as an email attachment. Porlock wrote a short note and clicked 'send'.

"I don't know why you bothered," Kate told him. "What does it matter when it was built?"

"Long shot? Hunch? Wycliffe seems to solve the most complex murders that way. Seriously though, there's something odd about that bridge which I can't quite put my finger on. I've a feeling it's important, though."

"Well, don't expect a reply any time soon."

But John Goldsmith came through on Porlock's mobile as they walked into a tunnel through the city walls. The bridge, Goldsmith told him, was almost certainly post-War, built perhaps in the late 1940s or early '50s. It may have been built on a wartime structure but he'd need a better picture to be sure. Kate took the phone and after a bit of small talk asked Mr Goldsmith to say hello to Rebecca.

They'd heard about a *trattoria* called the *Lion* near the Piazza San Salvatore. In fact it wasn't in the square but in a side alley. The door opened into a corridor between the bar and the open kitchen where they could see the cooks at work. They were seated in a small, perfectly square, room with pink walls and photograph-like pictures of well-dressed lovers. Four ceiling fans whirred above black mosquito nets. A party including a dozen children ate animatedly at tables joined together along one wall. At right angles to them was another long table of fifteen or so adults. Three members of the *polizia* sat close to them: a bald sergeant and two female lance corporals (at least, one-stripers) with large black automatic pistols and pigtails. The oil cloth on the tables was pink and blue, the chairs had straw seats.

They ordered *tagliatelle al ragu* and *verdure misti al forno* - (vegetables baked in an oven or furnace as Porlock guessed and Kate confirmed), followed by *torta di mele*, or apple tart, and *gelato alla crema* – Lucca laid claim to making the best ice cream in Tuscany, and Tuscany of course claimed to make the best in Italy.

Porlock asked for water. It was served in an elegant long necked carafe, and came from the fountain outside in Holy Saviour Square where people filled bottles under the statue of a woman in slipping robes. Water dripped into an enormous marble bath tub. It had a strange non-watery taste, not at all unpleasant.

Kate had half a bottle of red wine, chosen because she'd been told it was from the Tomlinson winery. Porlock read the label carefully and stared at the bridge logo. *Il Ponte Vecchio* the lettering above it said. "The Old Bridge," Kate translated. "There's one in Florence called that as well."

But Porlock wasn't listening – he was comparing the bridge on the bottle with the images on the screen of his camera. "I knew there was something odd about that bridge," he said at last. "Look for yourself. The bridges are different but the mountain scenery is the same, or very remarkably similar."

Kate took the bottle and clicked on the camera button to light up the screen again. She looked closely from one to the other for two minutes or so. "You're right, Joss, there's no doubt about that, but what does it tell us? What difference does it make?"

"There's writing underneath but it's too small to read," he

said. He picked up the bottle, pushing it away, pulling it closer to his eyes in an attempt to focus on the letters. "You don't have a magnifying glass, do you?"

"You do ask some weird questions at times, Joshua Porlock."

He looked around. A striking looking young woman wearing thick-lensed glasses sat with a girl friend in the corner. 'Dare I?' he asked himself, and decided 'no'. "Kate," he then said, "would you mind speaking to that young woman over there? The one with the thick glasses?"

"What for?"

"Ask her to take her glasses off and read the small print under the bridge logo on this label."

"Why?"

"I don't know. It might be nothing. If I go over she'll think it's the most kinky chat up line ever, and call on the *polizia* sitting next to us. They're packing heat."

"What makes you think she'll be able to read it if we can't?"

"Myopic people have eyes like microscopes."

Kate gave him a funny look but picked up the bottle and walked over to the corner. The young women looked up. Kate must have asked if they spoke English because he lip-read 'yes'. Then they both laughed when they realised what one of them was being asked to do. The short sighted one took off her glasses and held the bottle very close to her right eye like a jeweller, only without the loop. (Perhaps all short sighted people should work in the gem trade?) She began speaking as she put on her glasses again, at the same time handing the bottle back to Kate. "*Grazia*," he saw Kate say. "*Mille*."

She rejoined him, sat down, deliberately refilled her glass, and put the bottle back on the table. "Well?" he said. "Well?"

"You'll never guess."

"It says Rumpelstiltkin."

"No. You have two more guesses."

"But no patience. Please, Kate, what does it say?"

"Copyright Gideon Comely Estate'"

"Well, I'm damned," Porlock exclaimed. "I'll be absolutely, completely, utterly, and totally totally damned."

The *polizia* sergeant glanced at them for a moment, long

enough to convince him to speak quietly. The cop may or may not have understood English. They talked more quietly until they realised they were repeating themselves. "We have to tackle Tomlinson," Kate said.

"How?"

"His office must know where he is."

"Won't that be too dangerous? All we know about the Tomlinsons is that one of them is probably a criminal. A crook."

After they'd eaten they carried on talking it over as they walked in a quarter circle along the ramparts back to St Mary's Gate. On the battlements the trees drooped dustily in the hot dusk. The white walls of the Casa Cura di Santa Zita glowed a little in the late light. The last of the sun was touching the marble high up in the mountain quarries.

"Do we have a choice?" Kate asked. "What else can we do but tackle Tomlinson?"

"The wording on the label suggests the Estate is registered somewhere."

"Yes, in Italy. You're suggesting we take on the Italian bureaucracy?"

"It would be safer, and surer. Neither of the Tomlinsons, the young 'un or the old 'un, is hardly likely to admit to roguery."

"Yes, Joss, I know you're right but – don't you see? – the problem is we don't have enough Italian to talk technicalities to some bureaucrat in Florence or Rome, or wherever. And anyway it'd take months."

"The Embassy in London?"

"Solves the language problem but not the time one. If anything it'd extend it."

"Theoretically it could be done."

"Theoretically," Kate agreed.

"Well, yes, you're right, of course."

"We have to tackle the Tomlinsons."

"Head on?"

"How else?"

"Letter, phone, ambush?"

"Confront them, you mean? They might have a body guards."

"Kate!"

"They might. If they're involved in organised crime, they certainly will have."

"Kate, I just can't see Gideon being that important."

"Neither can I but we don't *know* who wants that painting or why."

"What if old man Tomlinson has a house here?"

"What if?"

"He'd have a private phone." By now they were alongside a High Renaissance Palazzo complete with playing fountains and statues in the back garden. They sat on a bench. "I'll ask the international operator," Porlock decided. "What have we got to lose?"

Porlock tapped the number for international enquiries into this mobile phone. "Yes, good evening. I'm looking for a number for a man called Tomlinson who lives somewhere in Tuscany in Italy. Probably near Lucca. No, I'm sorry, I can't be more precise, but it's an unusual name for Italy and I thought your computer might pick it up. It does? Yes, I do have a pen." He wrote down the number in the failing light. "Thank you. Thank you very much. You've been very helpful. Well," he turned to Kate, "we have a number."

"We already had a number – for the winery."

"Old Tomlinson must be in his eighties and retired."

"So? If young Tomlinson's involved, the winery must still be in the family. We could reach them that way."

"If we spoke to the old boy directly and in person we'd have no language problem, no second hand explanations."

"Joss, you're forgetting that we know at least one Tomlinson is a crook. How do we know both aren't? He may be old but that might just make him an elderly crook. A note might be safer."

"How good's the Italian postal service?"

"We could leave it at the winery. They could fax or email it."

"Just drop it in the letter box?"

"Why not? At least we'll know they've got it."

"Well," Porlock concluded, "we can compose a letter at least. No harm in that. We can use that computer in the hotel. Only five euros."

"Yes, that's best," said Kate. "We can make up our minds tomorrow. Don't mention the stolen painting. Keep it general. Five euros," she added. "It makes you wonder how can Italians afford to live in Italy?"

The left the battlements and walked down the ramp, through St Mary's Gate back to the hotel in the warm darkness. The computer was just inside the hotel lobby, with easy chairs, and a dedicated printer. "Dear Mr Tomlinson," Porlock typed. "Recently I was made aware that the Old Bridge logo you use on some of your brands is owned by the Gideon Comely Estate. I wonder if you could let me know where the estate is situated physically? My interest in Comely is as a painter, nothing else. He is completely unknown in his own country and, of course, if the owners of his estate wish him to remain so, that is fine. But from a purely personal point of view I wonder if it might be possible for me to see – look at, nothing more – some of his work?

Please let me apologise for putting you to any trouble, but if you could ask his Estate to entertain my request I'd be very grateful.

You can reach us – I am in Italy with a companion – either at the San Marco Hotel in Lucca or on my mobile, the number of which I attach below.

Once again, my apologies if you find this unreasonable, but all the same I look forward to hearing from you."

Kate put her glasses on to read it. "Any suggestions?" he asked.

"Yes," she said, taking off her glasses. "Yes, Joss, *yes*. what is the matter with us? We're just not thinking straight. Any business, even a very small one, must have somebody dealing with publicity. It would be perfectly all right to ask about something printed on their bottle labels. Wouldn't it?"

"We may not need to ask Tomlinson at all, you mean."

"No. And even if we do, we have a perfectly innocent reason for asking if the PR department passes it on. We just say we came across the painting on the wine bottle and would like to know more."

"Perfect alibi. Can we drive back up there tomorrow?"

"Why not? The company's main market is England. Any PRO they have must speak English."

"All the same, Kate, if the Tomlinsons are up to something shady we have to be circumspect."

"The staff are unlikely to be involved, are they?" Kate argued. "To them, it'll be just another question from the public."

"Right. We'll see if they have somebody dealing with publicity here in Italy. If not, we can phone the London office," I suppose.

"Well, that's more problematical. The answer's within a few miles of where we are, we do know that. Any way, let's take this letter with us."

"Why?"

"If the local press person can't answer, he can fax or email it to somebody who can."

CHAPTER 17

The local press person turned out to be a good looking young Italian woman who seemed to be bilingual. PR was only part of her job – she was also a guide. She was surprisingly vague about the logo but said she'd be pleased to phone Mr Tomlinson – yes, Mr Tomlinson senior – and read their letter to him. If he wanted to speak to them, he would: if not, she'd let them know – or they could drop in again tomorrow.

"We should let Margot know what's going on," Kate said. "To be on the safe side. If Tomlinson phones tell him people in England know where we are and expect to hear from us every hour."

"A fear of concrete overcoats?"

"Don't joke."

Porlock took out his phone. "It needs topping up."

"Use mine."

"Is the number in it?" he asked, taking it from her.

"Should be."

It was. "Hello, Joyce?" Porlock said when she answered. "Porlock here. Is Margot free? .... Ah, in that case can you take a message? .... It's to say we're in Italy and we may have located Gideon's painting. Stress may. We think Tomlinson's ... yes, the wine people – might know where it is exactly and we're expecting a call about it. The point is, we're a bit worried about organised crime over here which is why we'd like to keep in touch with you. If you don't hear from for some time, something will have gone wrong .... Nice of you say so, Joyce. Yes, you too, my handsome." He pressed the red icon to clear. "She says we're lovely people and not to get ourselves killed over a picture nobody's seen or thought for a hundred years."

"A hundred?"

"Getting on that way."

"It makes you wonder if this all worth the trouble. It isn't the Mona Lisa."

"It's worth it to me."

"In which case, what do we do until Mr Tomlinson phones?"

"Oh, that one's easy. We drive to Chianti."

So Kate drove into Chianti and its never ending ranges of blue hills – blue hills beyond blue hills below blue mountains. Blue hills and green valleys were what caught the eye and dominated the mind but it was a coloured country in other ways too: ochre and egg-yolk yellow walls of farms and their barns, red baked clay rooves and – along the waysides – rosemary with lavender-coloured flowers, lavender with mauve coloured flowers, and wild roses. As they drove they caught sight of snatches of aspen-coloured olive groves and long, combed lines of grape vines in paler green. On walls by the roadsides, poppies glowed bi-colouredly – red and then a deeper red where the translucent petals overlapped in the sun. They drove by purple vetch, white morning glory, and whole fields of yellow circled sunflowers all following the sun as though by clockwork.

But it was also a country of raw sienna, burnt sienna, raw umber, burnt umber – names taken from the city of Siena and the province of Umbria over the mountains to the east. These are the colours of the soil.

A tactile country too – surely? Those red tiles must be uplifting if touched, each with an evocative texture. Dry and brittle, also, overlapping each other by the million on barns and three-storey farm houses with outside stone stairs. Tiles, not slates: stone, not brick. They drove by barns with obsolete threshing floors outside and all the evocative (for Porlock) words which went with them – thresh, flail, winnow, husk, chaff. The guide books told him about shippens or byres with pottery troughs for watering animals. Everywhere they drove by shrines – Crucifixes or Madonnas with flowers and candles – as though mere belief had been made solid reality on earth.

Cypress trees were totemic, and almost always growing in straight lines. Non-native, of course. Who'd brought them? Etruscans? Romans? The Greeks had had colonies down the road: Pythagoras, the bean-shunning mystic had lived down that way with the Theorem.

Less often they came across *macchie* – the *maquis* of the

Resistance, surely? – spread out in great acres of thorns, home to wild sows, boars and piglets. Olive groves and vineyards were new to Porlock. Usually the vineyards were too far away to be seen clearly. Olive groves were closer, often growing right up to the verge. They surprised him most of all: he'd expected something like an English orchard or even a copse. Each tree here had its own space. They were also strangely thin and contorted into unearthly shapes like things in a folk tale or nursery story – branches and trunks writhed, twisted, looped and doubled back on themselves as though in agony. Almost all were new – not yet twenty years old – planted after one bad winter of frost had killed off the earlier ones.

Most of the time, Porlock was silent. Once he said: "It's a lift-off country, too, isn't it?" but didn't explain and Kate never asked. He meant that this landscape could easily lift you to that other, more universal, alternative world he sometimes visited.

Around noon, they stopped in a village for lunch. They sat outside the bar of the *albergo* under the shade of a trellis covered with ivy. Kate ordered *bruschetta* for both of them: discs of toasted Tuscan bread with olive oil, garlic, basil, tomatoes, red peppers and *proscuitto*. She had beetroot-red Chianti wine. He had a bottle of water.

"What was the population of Florence in the Renaissance?" Porlock asked rather absently.

"You're not asking me because you think I know, I hope?"

"No, not really," Porlock replied. "It's just that when you come to think about it, there have only been four true turning points in human history in the last two and a half thousand years: Athens, Galilee, Florence and Enlightenment and Industrial Revolution England. And *each* of them had extraordinarily small populations. Even in the late 17th century there couldn't have been more than a few million people in England. The others must have had populations in the tens of thousands. Yet look what they did and then look at us today – six billion mediocrities. Where's today's Dante and Michelangelo in the whole benighted lot of us?"

"Would you like something else? Cake? Coffee?"

"Coffee would be nice."

Kate took herself off back into the *albergo*.

War, Porlock thought: Etruscans, Romans, barbarians (Goths, Vandals?), Sienese, Florentines, German Holy Roman Emperors, Italian Popes – all warring for ownership, or overlordship, of Chianti. You could see the results all around in fortified farm houses with no ground floor windows. The British 8th and the US 5th Armies had passed that way in his own lifetime. "Remember that Harry Lime movie?" he asked Kate when she came back. "Italy had five hundred years of murder, bloodshed, war and tyranny. And produced the Renaissance. The Swiss had five hundred years of peace and brotherly love and invented the cuckoo clock."

Kate sat down, smiled, but said nothing. So far it hadn't been a day for much two-way conversation. A young woman came out with a tray. "*Cenci*," she said, unloading it. "*Pancosanti. Caffè.*"

"*Grazie*," said Kate in her best Italian.

"*Prego.*"

"*Pancosanti*?" Porlock queried. "Saint's bread?"

"Something like that. Bread with saints, more accurately."

"What a coincidence, wasn't it?" Porlock said, "that you booked into the same hotel as me back in England."

Kate looked at him. "What a lovely, simple, innocent man you are, Joshua Porlock."

Porlock in turn looked at her, with no understanding. "Oh?"

"The waitress by the harbour told you to go to Janice's art gallery."

"Yes. I remember," he said and added: "I see."

But Kate wasn't sure he did. She reached over to stroke his cheek.

After coffee, Porlock settled up and strolled off by himself while Kate, the sole driver, rested. The street through the village curved where the hills curved. Only one side was lined with houses: the other ended abruptly in a drop into a great green valley. Some houses were of undressed stone, others stucco'd and painted white or egg-yolk-yellow. Most had green louvred shutters, many of them shut against the heat which silenced the entire village. The paddle-shaped Post Office sign, glowing yellow like the sun itself, stuck out over the baking street. In places, trees threw blue shadows across the road and on to the houses. They made the hot shade a little less hot rather than cooler.

The outer walls of the church were a mix of russet and grey stone. Was the grey stone called *pietra serena*? Serene stone? A serenity of stone? Stone serenity? The church was seemingly built out in the empty space above the valley. The scooped out ceiling of the apse was filled with a painting, in need of restoring, of Christ enthroned with orb and sceptre, flanked by three Apostles and his earthly Mother. An inscription read: *Rex Regum Dominus Dominantium* which Porlock's old Latin master would have caned him for translating as 'the King rules, the Lord dominates', though it must mean something like that.

'Existence is such an oddity,' Porlock thought. 'It's such an odd thing, to be, to exist. Why do people baulk at an extra existence somewhere else yet don't bat an eyelid at the strange fact that they exist right here and now. We know we have this one, so why is another so unthinkable?'

Outside, small stone statues lined the path to the saint's grotto. One was of a child's head and shoulders. Her face was chubby and smiling and she had yellow spots of lichen on her long stone hair. The grotto, where the saint had lived, was a dusty, bone dry, narrow crack in the rock overlooking the green valley. Judging by her statue, she'd been a beautiful woman. Except it couldn't be her, of course: she'd lived in the 8th century. Perhaps this was a woman of the Renaissance? Whoever she was, Porlock stood next to her for a long while. Below them, the steep slope, dense with green bushes, ended in a brief plateau of olive groves bounded by an oak wood. Beyond lay the serene valley, green close in, blue towards the rise of hills and the darker blue mountains beyond, range after range, going on seemingly for ever. Across the valley, in the blue shade of the hills, he could just make out the lines of a vineyard, like scratches, below the blue and mauve hills. All was stilled by the heavy sunshine. The whole village was still, steeped in sunlight.

"Shall we go?" Kate asked when she caught up with him.

Porlock was reluctant. "Where to?"

"Nowhere in particular. Just drive. It's so beautiful here, it doesn't matter where we go."

"Not to the end of the Earthly Paradise?"

"No."

"No phone call as yet."

"There's still time."

The roads curved through olive groves and woods. Through openings they caught quick glimpses of pale green vineyards curving over the lower hills. And always beyond and all around were those blue hills, range after range of them, hill behind hill, their nearer crests a little ragged with the oak forests which cloaked them. Sometimes, beehives like painted boxes ran in a line around a hillside.

"You're not taking photographs?" Kate asked him.

"I keep forgetting to."

"You'll regret it later. No mementoes."

"I'll have to come back when I'm less transfixed."

"'Never go back' – who said that?"

"Somebody who'd never been to Tuscany, I'd imagine. Even Adam would have returned to Eden if he could have."

Eventually, in the late afternoon, Kate pulled up outside a castle on a ridge, a spur between two hollows, steep on either side. On both sides you looked down through Umbrian pines and fig trees to vineyards combed straight though curving over the contours. A farm building across the road from the castle had been converted into a ristorante. Ristorante was all it called itself but somebody had added, in a fine cursive script, *La sosta del gusto*.

"Kate?"

"Oh, dear. 'The pause of the taste'?"

"A literal translation, I take it?"

"Word for word."

"All the same, you get the drift. Sort of."

They ignored food and turned towards the cliff-like castle built of a beautiful golden stone, uncrenelated but with an overhanging turret at one end with holes for, presumably, pouring boiling olive oil down on the unfriendly. Yet why would anybody want to climb a hundred foot wall under a shower of hot oil when, by strolling twenty yards to the right, the top of the wall was clear of battlements? Somebody would know but Porlock, the ever curious, was incurious for once.

Two coach parties were just pulling away and so, apart from a few couples, they had the run of the place for a few minutes. Little in Italy was free and the entrance fee to the castle was five euros apiece. But those ten euros let them go back through ten centuries as they stepped into the square courtyard. On two of the four sides were porticos with arches and grey stone pillars. *Pietra Serena* again? A serenity of stone to calm the heart and lift the soul in an age of emptiness? Porlock felt too old to be brow-beaten any longer by tiresome Baby Boomers who were too materialistic to be complete.

The few windows around the courtyard were well above ground level, each rimmed with soft grey stone. Most were arched but one, right up under the eaves was square: an empty hanging flower basket hung outside it. The wall of one portico was hung with bygone vineyard and olive grove tools. What they were for you could only guess at – among them some kind of scoop-bladed spade and what looked an adze but was probably a hoe. The sickle was obvious, along with a saw and what must have been pruning shears. A wooden chest stood in one portico, with a table and a vase of flowers next to a rough-hewn timber door. The castle's well was next to a 'stone of serenity' pillar. A huge iron wheel would have been used to winch up the buckets. (If the castle had piped water now, where did it come from?) A sink next to the well was filled with flowers. A Medici owned the place once.

Inside, enormous stone fireplaces were stacked with logs from the oak forests on the hills all around. Small-paned windows gave limited views of sunlight on Umbrian pines and nothing else. The ceilings were wooden beamed. Arches and balustraded stairs led to the upper floors passed iron framed windows. In the silence of thick stone walls, lingered the scent of last winter's wood smoke.

'There's something spiritual about continuity time and stillness,' Porlock thought. 'Stillness and sunlight on stone.'"

Why not just give up and stay here, lost in the melancholy of olive groves and history? He could make a photographic study of Chianti, a view through a foreign eye, the insight of a man who sometimes saw through time.

At the back of a huge open fireplace, in what must have been the kitchen, was a tiny window close to where the flames would have been. Why there? Why didn't the glass crack? The stone oven was like a small cave, not much smaller in fact than the grotto, in which the saint had lived, in the village where they'd had lunch. Sunlight fell on an ancient flag-stoned floor. A frieze of red flowers with green stalks ran around one entire room.

They went back outside and across the road on to a bed of soft pine needles on what turned out to be a terrace with a drop of thirty feet or so. Porlock stared at the receding ranges of blue hills. Oak forest came down to the valley floor, hemming in a small vineyard. He moved along the terrace in front of the castle until he could look at the blue hills through sun-translucent fig leaves, thick-fingered fig leaves hanging sun greened. A row of close-set pines grew along the edge of the narrow road curving around the bend. On the far right, the tips of cypress spires rose high enough to be lit by the sun while the bottom halves were in the shade.

Farther along, the edge of the terrace ended in a long down-slope. Pines grew on it. The sun was settling behind the mountains, turning them dark mauve, and scattering light through the needles on the trees, its rays then streaming in long lines over the grass and fallen pine needles of the terrace, throwing the shadows of leaves on the old stone walls of the castle.

It had been one of the deepest days of Porlock's life, never to be repeated, relived or even properly remembered. The earth itself had been transformed into something more aetherial, less solid, for hours on end and quite unlike the usual dissolution which lasts only seconds. "Sun's going down," he said when Kate joined him.

"Yes."

"No phone call."

"There's still time," Kate consoled him. "Shall we drive on?"

"Where to?"

"Florence is only six or seven miles away."

"Should we go to an important place like Florence just to kill time there?"

"We'll see it after dark," Kate said, inconsequentially.

It was dark by the time they reached the Medieval bridge, il

Ponte Vecchio, lined with shops where parapets would normally have been. The shops were all aglitter with gold, the hot air outside the windows heated by the lamps which made the gem stones shine more brightly. A police car was parked obliquely across the road at the Oltrarno end. City police in white helmets talked to anybody who wanted to talk to them. Below, the Arno flowed on to Pisa and the sea. Between the shops on the bridge they could see Fiesole on its tumulus-like hill, glittering now with strings of lights.

Crowds milled in the hot air, making the night even hotter with radiated body heat. A string trio – guitar, violin and double bass – played in the Square of the Republic. The pavement tables were full, and the narrow lanes – canyons – seethed with people. Porlock and Kate found an empty table in a *gelateria* and asked for cones piled high with mango and chocolate ice cream. The woman behind the bar – smouldering, sultry – would have looked more at home in a Fellini film than an ice cream parlour. Police, packing guns, drank coffee standing at the counter.

"What will you do when this all over?" Kate asked.

"Well, there's supposed to be a plateau in the South American rain forest with sheer unclimbable walls on all sides. There's no way up and only water comes down, in enormously long falls. On top, untouched rainforest steams in the clouds and the heat. Can you imagine it? The Lost World of the Victorians. They thought dinosaurs might still live there. Unless it's fiction, of course."

"You'd hate it."

"How do you know?"

"I do know. Florence is more you."

"The Brownings lived here."

"Well?"

"I never liked either of them."

"Well?"

"E M Forster wrote a book partly set in Florence. In the Edwardian period, I think. *A Room with a View.*"

"Did you like it?"

"It's silly in places – Forster was little more than a boy when he wrote it – but it has its moment. It's about the necessity of living in accordance with the nature of things."

"Oh, dear. As bad as that?"

"I'm afraid it's also about expelling God from the Garden of Eden and reinstating Adam and Eve, which rather contradicts Forster's idea about obeying the nature of things. The Florentine half doesn't work but the Surrey bits are not too bad. That was because, I suspect, he was an outsider in Tuscany but an insider in Surrey. His description of the Surrey Hills and The Weald is almost spiritual even though he was an atheist. It's strange really because his deepest thought seems to have been expressed in a simple motto – 'only connect' – connect, presumably, with the nature of things as well as with other people. Yet he himself failed to connect with his own spiritual insight, if in fact that's what it was. Clever but not clever enough, I'd say. More charitably – clever but incomplete. A lot of very intelligent people are, aren't they?"

"I don't know," said Kate, finishing her *gelato*. "I've never thought about things like that."

"The book's also partly about a young man who's incomplete in another kind of way – he knows the inside of books but not people."

"And is that you?"

"I know neither books nor people, Kate. To me, there's something extra, something more, something of the utmost importance, though what it is you can never really tell and never completely grasp."

"What can be more important to a person than people?"

"Well, that something extra can be – to a certain type of personality, obviously. Not everybody. One or two in a million?" In turn, Porlock finished the huge ice cream. "Do you think anybody will phone?"

"You can't expect people to drop everything right away just to please you."

"No?"

"No. A last cup of coffee?"

"Yes, why not?" He went over to the bar, ordered, paid for and collected *due cappuccini*. The policeman made room for him.

"Why don't we move to Florence for a few days?" Kate said when Porlock came back with the two cups.

"I'd love to live in Tuscany permanently," Porlock said

obliquely, "but it's really a question of belonging, isn't it? You have to be born in a place like this to belong. E M Forster makes the case for me. He belonged in Surrey but not in Italy and it showed. There's too much history here, too much continuity, too much spirituality for an outsider to fit in."

"Some people can always fit in anywhere."

"Some people?"

"Simple people."

"Shallow people?"

"Simple is nicer."

"You called them shallow a couple of days ago."

"Uncomplicated is kinder."

"How many people do you think are spiritual?" he asked with a Kate-like switch of subjects.

"Almost nobody is, not in my experience. Not today."

"Not even the religious ones?"

"Particularly them."

"Michelangelo," Porlock went on, "was a Platonist who disagreed with Plato. About art anyway. Art to Plato was a bad thing because it copied what was only a copy of the real thing up there in a realm beyond the sky. Not so, says Michelangelo, art is a freeing – an opening up to view – of the real, eternal thing up there wherever it is. I'm with Michelangelo on this one, particularly as the same applies to time and landscape. E M Forster was never able to understand that."

Kate finished her coffee first: she always did, liking it hot, while Porlock was a lingerer. "It's getting late," she said. "We'd better be getting back."

"Yes, of course."

"We can come back tomorrow."

"Yes, of course. Unless there's a phone call."

"Of course." As the stepped out into the narrow lane, she added: "You're not going to South America, by the way."

"Oh?"

"No. And you can 'Oh?' as much as you like"

"Can we get a shot of the cathedral before we go?"

"Joshua, you really are the limit at times. You've taken no photographs all day and now, when I'm tired and want to go to bed, you get the urge."

"It's been a good day," Porlock said. "I think I've found my niche in life, you know. Photographs of places. There's a depth below things which you can capture in images."

"So why didn't you start when you were young?"

"No confidence, I suppose. I didn't think I could either compete with others or do things well. The old cameras were a bit off-putting too – f-stops and focal lengths, and different types of film for different types of light, and so on. Snobbery too, probably – photography is hardly an art form, or is it?"

"I think it is. And what a shame you didn't take it up years ago. You have a painter's eye."

"But not a painter's patience or skill with a brush. All that mixing to get the colours right can't be easy either."

"See? There you go again. Always negative. You need pushing, my boy."

"The idea would be to publish a whole bookful of pictures, perhaps with short poems – if I could write any – like Japanese haiga. A chap in Scotland does something similar. I'd like to go to Japan. You'd have no objections, would you?"

"Not to Japan, no. Japan might be good for you. We could go together. But first you need a bungalow with a big shed or something for a studio, or workshop."

"No, I don't."

"We're getting somewhere now, I think."

"We're getting close to the Duomo, that's where we're getting."

For a time they strolled around the Medieval cathedral, clad in Victorian marble. Porlock lined up a night shot of the Bell Tower and Baptistery with the red-tiled dome in the background. He widened the angle to take in the crowds and the lights on the right – the brightly lit *caffès* and the dimmer lights in the apartments above.

Just as he pressed the button, his phone went off. He dropped the camera, letting it swing on the loop around his wrist, the lens still protruding, as he fumbled in his shirt pocket for the phone. It only ever rang a few times before switching to voice mail. The phone had slipped sideways and jammed. In desperation, he jerked it out, scattering pens and a recently bought, folded, street map of Florence. "Hello?"

CHAPTER 18

"**M**r Joshua Porlock?"

"Speaking."

"Harry Tomlinson."

The phone emphasised a barely detectable West Country burr, something which Porlock (unrealistically) associated with honesty. (What about all those wreckers, smugglers and pirates?) He relaxed a little. "Thank you for calling, Mr Tomlinson," he said. "You got my note?"

"No. I'm in Rome. It was read to me over the phone. You're interested in Gideon Comely?"

Burr or no burr, Porlock was wary again. "Yes."

"Mr Porlock, if we're going to spar with each other we'll be here till midnight. Do you know of a painting called *Gideon's God*."

"Yes," Porlock admitted, taken aback.

"What do you know about it?"

"It's stolen."

"Ah." Tomlinson sounded as if a suspicion had been confirmed. "You know that for a fact?"

"Yes."

"Not forged?"

"Forged?" Porlock was startled. "No, certainly not."

"Do you know who stole it?"

"We've a good idea but I imagine Italy has slander laws the same as everywhere else."

"Who are you, Mr Porlock?"

"Nobody, Mr Tomlinson. I'm not the police, or a private detective, or an insurance investigator. I'm a retired civilian who began all this by wanting to see *Gideon's God* for purely private reasons. I traced it to its owner, but it was stolen before I had a chance to look at it."

"You know its owner?"

"Yes."

"Are you acting on his behalf?"

Porlock hesitated over the 'his'. "No," he said, "but the owner knows we're here and that we're in contact with you. We're in touch regularly." Kate nodded approval and gave the thumbs up sign. "Do you know where the painting is, Mr Tomlinson?"

"I'll make enquiries. I'm not involved, by the way, if that's what you thought."

"It had crossed my mind."

"Can I get back to you?"

"Of course."

"On this number?"

"That would be best."

"Later tonight then."

"I'll expect your call."

Tomlinson hung up. Porlock checked that he had, then carefully switched off the receiving end of his mobile.

"Did you get the gist of that?" he asked Kate.

"Partly."

"We're getting somewhere. He knows about *Gideon's God*."

"What does he know?"

"I don't know. I think he knows where it is. He's calling back. Tonight, hopefully."

"Is he involved?"

"He says not."

"We can't be sure."

"He has a West Country accent underneath a posh one."

"Well?"

"Well, nothing really."

They drove back to Lucca in the dark and were just parking outside their hotel when the phone rang again. "If I give you an address," Tomlinson said, "could you be there by ten-thirty or eleven o'clock tomorrow morning? It's a thirty minute drive from Lucca."

"Yes, of course."

"Do you have a pen and paper handy?"

"One moment." Porlock switched on the roof light and took out the map of Florence and a pen from his shirt pocket. "Ready."

"I'll spell it."

Porlock wrote it down. "Can you tell me more?"

"No."

"And *Gideon's God*? Is it there? At this address?"

"Just go there, Mr Porlock." And he hung up.

Porlock held up the map with the address written on it. "He wants us to go to this place between 10.30 and 11 o'clock tomorrow morning."

"All right. So far so good." She switched off the roof light. They sat in the dark in the green glow of the dashboard. "Phone Margot," she said. "Tell her that of she doesn't hear from us by noon tomorrow, something bad has happened."

"You're serious?"

"Never more so."

Next morning they were the first guests at breakfast. Porlock was too nervous to eat: nervousness led Kate to eat too much. "Have a bread roll," she urged him. "You must eat something. We don't know when we'll eat again."

"At times like these I can't face food."

"At times like these I can't stop eating. Have some bread at least. Coffee isn't enough."

It was lovely morning which went unnoticed, as did the landscape, so there was no need to drive slowly. They bought a street map of the town, found the public toilets (and used them) and parked around the corner at 10.10. They waited. Porlock looked at his watch. "Still time to engage first gear and drive away."

"No." She opened the driver's door and got out. "Come on."

They were in a broad street of rather grand houses, well shaded with trees: pines like sixty foot mushrooms forked into twin trunks at around twenty feet. Most of the houses were late 19th century, with that air of permanence and perpetual sunshine. All were detached. One had a bay window as big as a small room. Its stained glass panes were moulded into flowing shapes by elegant swirling ironwork. Above them, sunflowers were painted in a great oval on either side of the louvred window or door opening on its balcony. Why? Who would want to sit or stand there?

The house they were looking for was only two storeys high. It was painted lemon yellow with a frieze of white flamingos under the eaves. Bamboos as big as trees grew in the small walled garden between house and road. The street number (no house seemed to have a name) was written in beautifully written numerals in Spanish azure blue on a tile set in the gatepost. Stone-balustraded steps curved up to a tall rather narrow door with an old-fashioned bell-pull. Porlock pulled it, raising his eyebrows and looking at Kate as he did so. "Folly?" he said.

The door opened within seconds. Two men stood there. Both stepped out, forcing Kate and Porlock back down on to the path. One, the burlier, was turning grey. The other was younger, probably in his late twenties. Both were big and they now had the advantage of looking down on Porlock and Kate from the top of the steps. "Porlock?" the older man said to Kate.

"No," she told him very firmly. "Mrs Finch."

"Porlock?" he said to Porlock.

"Yes, Porlock," Porlock agreed.

"You bring painting?"

"No," said Porlock, "we haven't brought anything. We're looking for a painting." He pointed to his eyes.

"You bring painting?" he asked again.

The younger man said: "Brought, Papa."

"You brought painting?"

"No. We have never had the painting." (God, Porlock thought, the intricacies of English syntax are going to be the death of us.) "We're *looking* for a painting. A stolen one."

"*Stiamo cercando una pittura rubata*," Kate added, helpfully.

The older man hesitated – was he going to try to frisk them? – and if so, what could Porlock do? – then he made up his mind and called through the door: "*E tutto bene, zietta. Sono vecchi. Inoffensiv*i."

"What a cheek," Kate said indignantly. "He says we're old and harmless. He's also talking to his auntie."

"Do the Mafia have God-Aunties?" Porlock asked.

The older man turned back to them. "The Signora see you. *Non siamo lontano*," he added, pointing at himself and the younger man.

"He's warning us they won't be far away," Kate translated. She held up her mobile phone. "*Dobbiamo telefonare da mezzogiorno.*"

Porlock was impressed. The older Italian smiled (was Kate's syntax as mangled as his English?). Both then stood aside to make way for the Signora.

CHAPTER 19

The Signora stood in the open doorway – tall, slim, elegant, around seventy, leaning on a ebony walking cane. Apart from that, only the lines on her face showed she was no longer a young woman, or at least a much younger one. She was an unusually arresting figure but, for Kate, there was to her than that – there was something familiar about her. Had they met sometime, somewhere? Hardly likely – Kate had lived most of her life in Merton, South London.

"My nephew and great nephew," she introduced the two men. "My family are over-protective." She spoke unaccented English with, disconcertingly, Italian gestures. " I am Carla Simonetti." Porlock, although a bit stunned, still had enough presence of mind to introduce himself and Kate. Carla acknowledged them and spoke privately to her nephew and his son. Reluctantly they agreed to go, though probably not *lontano*. Then she gave her full attention to what were now, it seemed, her guests. "Mr Tomlinson told me you want to see Gideon Comely's paintings."

"One painting," Porlock corrected her. "We had no idea there were others."

"And that is the one we don't have. Please do come in, though. We have a little gallery here. We're fortunate in having the space. We're a very large family. "

Porlock and Kate looked at each other. Porlock shrugged and raised his hands in a gesture which said: "How could I have known it'd be like this?" But Kate glared at him with a look which said: "It's all your fault. You should have known."

The gallery was a long whitewashed narrow room in a cool part of the house. Soft white light filtered through a shaded window at one end, as well as shaded skylights in the sloping roof. An old fashioned padded bench, for viewing the paintings, stood in the middle. Paintings hung on three walls with windows along the fourth – a miniature replica of the Old Ballroom Gallery. Carla sat on the bench.

It was extraordinary: a whole gallery devoted and dedicated to a single artist – Gideon Comely. The only thing anything like which Porlock could recall was the Watts gallery in Surrey, and that was falling apart. Porlock was totally taken up with the paintings but Kate, from time to time, looked at Carla in a puzzled kind of way. 'Something about her rings a bell,' Kate thought. No point in asking Porlock: by now she knew him well enough not to expect him to be observant – not when it came to people: ideas and landscapes, yes: people, no.

Most of Gideon's paintings, it turned out, were figurative but idiosyncratic: Gideon had always been his own man. A particularly fine one was of a woman in a shawl and apron carrying a baby in front of a church with a campanile and – what would you call it? A porch? A portico? The pillars were thin at the bottom, thick at the top; strange and seemingly the wrong way around. The church was a beautiful pale yellow with an unnaturally dark blue sky behind it.

Next to it was an unusual still-life, if living fruit can be called still: green grapes growing on a vine as seen against the sun, more like a camera angle than a painting's. If painted in the open air it must have been dangerous to his eyes. Rays like a halo circled the grapes some of which were translucent with sunlight, shading them from green to a riper yellow.

There was only one townscape – a clean, narrow, gold-coloured street with no roadway, just a pavement between old stone buildings. It was evening, but the sky was still light blue. Lamps were strung on wires down the middle of the street, bringing out the yellowness of the stone. One, high in the foreground, shone like a guiding star. Yellow was a favourite colour. Yellow, in all its shades, and blue.

Another painting was of a hillside, rich with violets pouring down like dark blue water. Porlock had seen something similar in an oak wood on a fellside in Westmorland. Only there the flowers had been bluebells. He'd mistaken them for flowing water. Gideon's painting, too, caught that sense of movement.

The paintings of his last years were almost entirely landscapes. To Porlock's surprise, three or four seemed to be of places they'd driven past yesterday: places which he too would have chosen to paint if he'd been a painter.

"This castle," Porlock said, standing in front of one painting, "I'm sure we drove there yesterday. How did Mr Comely get about?"

"Natasha drove him everywhere in an old open-topped tourer. Some landscapes he painted while sitting in the back of the car with the roof half up like a sun shade. Some, we think, are from photographs which Natasha took on those old glass negative plates. Gideon then worked them into paintings when he was 'down' and not fit to go out. He never really stopped working, in spite of being down quite a lot."

"Down?" said Kate.

"Shell shock. From the War."

"He never got over it?"

"No, not really, though he was getting better. It was so sad that he was killed on one of his good days. Natasha had driven them out into Chianti for a day's painting. Not far from your castle, Mr Porlock, as it happens."

"He did the Florence sights, I see," said Porlock. "The *Ponte Vecchio*."

"In his own unconventional way he was a religious man. He saw religious meanings in old unbroken things."

"In landscape, too, I shouldn't wonder," Porlock added.

"Do you have a photograph of him?" Kate wanted to know.

"Yes. We have an album. If you're interested, I can show it to you."

"I'd love to see it," said Kate. "Mr Porlock recently bought a camera," she went on. "The pictures he takes are the same kind as these. They're like kindred spirits." Porlock, embarrassed, held out his hands in a questioning gesture. All the same, Kate was right. It was as though Gideon and he had the same eye, saw the same sights, had the same insights and got the same sense of a Great Elsewhere out of sunlight on walls and landscape.

Only one painting stood out because it was so different. It looked like a painting of a brown sea in late evening, with light slanting down from behind the spectator. Light glinted off small waves under a dark sky. He was looking at with a growing awareness of what it was and what it showed when

Kate called him over. She stood in front of a painting of the bridge.

"Is this the original of the bridge logo on all those wine bottles?" Porlock asked, pointing to it.

"The same bridge," Carla conceded, "but a different painting. The one next to it is the one the winery use for their logo."

He stepped sideways to look at it. "But this is a reproduction."

"There's a reason for that, as well as a very strange story." Carla stood up. "I take it, then, Mr Porlock, that you like my father's paintings?"

"Father?" This from Kate.

"Gideon Comely?" Porlock asked, as though for confirmation.

"Your *father*?"

"Would you like tea or coffee?" Carla asked in her most civilised manner. "In the kitchen?"

She led the way, talking as she went. "It's a very modern kitchen. My children – Gideon Comely's grandchildren – insist on that. The place is usually seething with them, or their children, our extended family and all their friends. You've caught me in a slack moment." The kitchen was not only modern but large. It comfortably held a family-sized table and a breakfast bar. Ovens were set into the wall itself. Hobs seemed, to Porlock at least, to be part of the draining board or work top. One wall was almost entirely window. It opened onto a formal Tuscan garden with a terrace and a table long enough for a whole extended family to eat together in the shade. Beyond it lay a garden more wild and natural in its layout.

"Would you prefer tea. Mr Porlock?" she asked. "Englishmen often do."

"No, thank you. Just coffee, please."

Down one side of the garden there are a long extension, like an elongated granny flat, expensively stucco'd and painted the same lemon yellow as the house. On the other side a six foot wall kept them private. In the grounds itself were what looked to Porlock like banana plants and orange trees. Carla and Kate came back out with the cups, coffee pot and a cream jug.

At first Kate did most of the talking, filling in the background – the old artists' colony and the island, Margot and the new art gallery, the theft of the painting and what she and Porlock had done about it.

"A Mr Maddox isn't behind it all, is he?" Carla asked

"Possibly," said Kate.

"Kate's being cautious. We're pretty sure he is." Porlock then told Carla about their evening in Anson's.

"Gabriel Tomlinson, as well?" said Carla. "I'm genuinely sorry to hear that. He's Major Tomlinson's son."

"We wondered at one time if the Major was involved as well."

"No.' This was said with a simple finality which ended the matter. "Mr Maddox wanted to buy some family land I have on the coast. He said he wanted to develop it as a holiday complex. Up-market, he called it. Poor man. I felt sorry for him. He was so much out of his depth. This is Italy and he doesn't even speak the language."

"But why would they steal *Gideon's God*?" Porlock wanted to know.

"A sweetener? An inducement? A bribe? A goodwill gesture? Proof of good intent? A way of saying we're civilised people? They'd certainly done their homework and gone to a lot of trouble. First of all they knew of my family's interest in Gideon Comely's work, though not that he was my father. Then, they'd gone to the trouble of creating a false provenance."

"A young Italian lad – a man, really – was also involved," Kate said. "Perhaps he knows you."

"Very likely. Major Tomlinson has some ideas about that. He's looking into it."

"You've seen the picture?"

"No. I've seen the provenance. Mr Maddox brought it. It was convincing, except now I know the painting is stolen."

"Would giving you the picture have worked?" Porlock wanted to know. "I mean, realistically? It sounds a bit – what – lightweight?"

"It warmed me to Mr Maddox. To that extent it worked. It was very good way of introducing himself. I'm sure he'll go on to make a lot of money, if that's what he wants. And we have no use for the land. It's the size of a pocket handkerchief and a swamp more than anything else. I don't think it's worth developing but of course I'm no expert. I'd have felt it dishonest to sell, particularly to a foreigner. We're not a poor family and Italians rarely sell what they inherit."

"Did your father ever talk about the island?" Kate asked with one of her characteristic changes of subject.

"Not to me. But then he died when I was only four or five. Natasha never really spoke about their life in England. I think she just wanted to put the War behind them and start again here in Italy. She did say he'd burned all his work – which, of course, was the main reason we thought the painting was a forgery. And then he died so stupidly. He was accidentally wounded by some stupid hunters, shooting little birds, of all things. Not a serious wound, but we had no antibiotics in those days. That's one thing about my country which I do hate so much. Why do they have to shoot little song birds?"

Kate began to speak, hesitated, and finally said: "Was Natasha your mother?"

"Natasha was my father's *wife*. She couldn't have children. My mother was Italian – the reason I have such deep roots here."

Porlock asked how Major Tomlinson fitted into this scheme of things and Carla told them the extraordinary story of how their lives had become so intermixed. Then a telephone rang. "Excuse me," she said, fishing in a bag she carried around her neck. She brought out a extension phone. She spoke rapidly in Italian, then listened. "*In ritardo dieci minuti?*" She looked up at the clock on the kitchen wall. "*Si, si,*" she concluded "I'm sorry," she said to them in English. "I'd forgotten I have some business to look after. But we have a lot more to talk about. I'd like your opinion of my father's work and also Harry – Major Tomlinson – would like to meet you."

"We're here for a few days," Kate said.

"Till we find that lost painting," Porlock added.

Carla took their phone numbers and then told them of a ristorante in Garibaldi Square. "Tell Giuseppe I sent you otherwise he'll give you the tourists' menu and not the one for locals. He was a rogue as a boy and he's still a rogue at fifty. And no cover charge, tell him. It's illegal in Italy."

******

"And you think I'm bossy," said Kate as they walked to the piazza in the mid-day heat. "Goodness, she makes me feel dowdy and .... what's the word?"

"Provincial?"

"Possibly. Have you taken an aspirin?"

"What on earth for?"

"The heat. Heat thickens the blood, aspirin thins it. At least let's walk in the shade." Across the street it was only a little cooler, but much easier on the eyes. Piazza Garibaldi was surprisingly small: the outside tables of the ristorante, Osteria Aristo, filled a good quarter of it. It was secluded, quiet and clean. An Italian flag hung down from a pole on one building. Garibaldi himself made his appearance as a bust on a plinth in the centre. Porlock had only ever seen him in heroic poses but here his beard, moustache and drooping eyebrows made him look melancholy and depressed. *All Eroe dei due monde, Agosto 1884*. Kate translated: "To the hero of the two worlds."

"Two worlds? What does that mean?" he asked but Kate didn't know either. Giuseppe came over to greet them. "*Signora Carla ci inviati*." It was like a magic wand changing Giuseppe from a man intent on fraud into an honest one.

"Did you see him switch menus?" Kate asked Porlock.

"No."

"Well, he did." Porlock was silent. "Poor Joss. You just want to be alone, don't you?"

"How do you know that?"

"I'm getting to know you very well. Why don't you go for a walk. By yourself."

"Well, if you don't think it's rude?"

"Shoo. Take a stroll around the square. Two or three times."

"If you don't mind and don't think I'm neglecting you?"

"Go. Shoo."

Porlock walked around Garibaldi, that man of action, two or three times and then sat on a bench overhung by some kind of flowering bush. The square was surprisingly quiet. Perhaps heat does dampen down noise, he thought. The idea of his room in the inn with its view of lichened stone was attractive but it was a thousand miles away. Somebody else probably had it by now. What was happening was astonishing – but did he deserve it and would he spoil it with some stupid blooper? (*Blooper*? Where did that come from? Had he made it up?) What he wanted, he realised, was quietness – activity recollected in Wordsworthian tranquillity – but for that you had to have had action beforehand. He was a contemplative, a theoriser, a deviser of overviews. For that you had to be a collector of ideas, experiences, facts. Only his experience of that strange Elsewhere was completely individual, totally disconnected from everybody else, unlearned, unlearnable, too deep for speech. Everything else was pretty second hand. Yet people were pack-mammals and even Porlock – a solitary, if ever there was one – needed contact of some kind. He couldn't afford a loss of nerve, a characteristic shying away, a burrowing down. This was his last chance to fill in the long emptiness. Giving way now would be the greatest of all the great refusals in a life never truly lived.

Even so, resolved as he was, he almost faltered when he got back to the *ristorante*. Kate said: "Carla rang. Would we like to have dinner this evening with her and Major Tomlinson? At his home. Address given. I said yes. Is that all right?"

"Haven't we done enough for one day?"

"No. You've just begun. You can't stop now." She looked at him. "I'll be there."

Had the surge of fear-driven resolution which had carried him this far – selling up, setting out – at last petered out? Was he reverting to type? Porlock looked at the menu, the one for locals. "Where does the Major live?"

"In sight of the bridge."

"We must have passed it in pursuit of Jolly Jack."

"I wasn't looking at the scenery, you may remember."

There was no way back, he told himself and: "We have to press on, don't we?"

"Yes."

"No turning back?"

"No."

"So," Porlock resolved. "a light lunch, back to the hotel, shower, rest, change and then head for the hills?"

"That's my boy." In turn, Kate picked up the menu and began to read. "Isn't Major Tomlinson's story extraordinary? You wouldn't have thought such things could happen."

"We should email the landlady of *The Crown and Anchor*. She'd be astonished to learn why Tomlinson's *tavola* comes from Tuscany."

CHAPTER 20

Flashback: 1944

The fighting had been intense, hand to hand at one stage and what looked like rust on his knife was in fact dried blood. Directly across the valley, a mile away through clear sir, a walled city on a hill was still in the shadow of the Tuscan Apennines. He, on the other hand, was already lit by the rising sun. A bell in the campanile of the cathedral tolled the quarter hour. He checked his watch. The clock was slow. A monastery – commandeered by the Germans, as he knew from the briefings – was high on the mountain behind him. Between them, monastery and town had controlled the bridge on its high, slender piers in the valley. He'd heard the crumps of their explosives hours ago: the charges had gone off – but was the bridge down?

"Over here." Tomlinson turned over on to his back, automatically working the bolt of his Sten gun. Square in his sights was the chest of a gawky young girl in a worn pink frock. She flung her arms in the air in the gesture of surrender. "Come with me," she said in perfect English. He put up the gun and stood in a single movement. "Come on," she said again. "It's all right."

They ran crouching double along a narrow path through mixed woods of oaks and chestnuts. At times, surely, they were in sight of the sentries on the ramparts of the town? Light flickered on his khaki battle dress, and the girl's faded pink frock, as they ran. Then the path turned right along the contours of a side valley taking them out of the line of sight of the sentries. The girl stopped to catch her breath, smiling at the soldier as she pointed to a cave in the rock of the hillside above them. "No," said Tomlinson. "The Germans will search it."

"Come on," she said, unperturbed by his refusal, and ran over a stone bridge across a stream and along the hillside, briefly back into the sunlight in sight of the city on its hill. A convoy of Wehrmacht lorries passed along the road down in the valley. Behind them, foot patrols in field grey spread out in the forest.

The girl slowed. By the time they reached the turning into a farm, she was struggling for breath. In the farm yard was a long orange painted house. Joined to the house was a barn with its doors wide open. The child pointed to it, then doubled over, hands on her knees, to get her breath. Tomlinson looked warily around, finger on the trigger. It was early: that beautiful southern light was rising. Two rather scrawny hens clucked and scratched. He thought he heard a pig squeal. Somebody, long ago, had painted Mussolini's face on the barn wall, along with a slogan. Childlike, the girl was soon breathing more normally and straightened up. Again she pointed to the barn and began calling "Mamma. Natasha." Tomlinson stepped inside the barn and waited by the door with the Sten's safety catch off.

Almost immediately the child was back with two women. They were almost silhouetted against the bright morning. He pushed the safety catch on, then pointed the gun at the ground. He wouldn't kill them whatever they intended. "You're safe here," one of them said in perfect English. "We can hide you."

"The Germans will shoot you if they find me here," he reminded them. "And if you turn me in the Fascists will give you a reward."

"Nearly two thousand lira," the other women said in accented English.

"Your Army will be here soon," said the first woman. "The war in Italy is nearly over. I'm Natasha," she introduced herself, "and this is Maria. She is Carla's mother, and this is Carla." The girl smiled beautifully and bobbed a little curtsy.

Tomlinson held out his hand. "Thank you, Carla," he said. "You're a brave girl. I'm Harry Tomlinson," he added.

"Captain Tomlinson," Natasha said, looking at the three pips on his epaulets. "Carla's father was a Captain in the English Army in the last War."

Captain Tomlinson shook hands with Carla's mother. "You're welcome to my house," she said, in imperfect English.

Natasha had gone to the back of the barn. "Fortunately," she called over, "this is a very old place and it's seen a lot of troubles." They all three joined her. She pointed at a trapdoor. "And so it has a hideaway, if you'll help me." Tomlinson helped her lift the trapdoor which opened into a deep cellar. Tomlinson shook his head. "The Germans will search it," he said.

"Inside there's a door which opens into a little cell. They won't find that." Natasha found an oil lamp. "Have you a match." He took a box from the breast pocket of his battle dress blouse and gave it to her. Maria went to the door to keep a look out. Natasha wiped dust off the lamp's glass chimney, raised it, and lit the wick. It burned smokily yet threw strange shadows as Natasha led the way to the back wall of the cellar. "Somewhere, somewhere, somewhere," Natasha repeated, running her hand down one of two baulks of timber set into the wall.

Maria ran up the mouth of the cellar. "Hurry, hurry," she called down to them, then ran back to the door.

Tomlinson propped his Sten gun against the wall. "If they catch us," he told Natasha, "pick this up and make out you've taken me by surprise and captured me. If you hand me over, they won't hurt you."

"Be quick," Maria called over, now with panic in her voice. "They are coming." They could hear shouted orders. With great presence of mind Maria shut the barn door. It couldn't be locked but it delayed the Germans for a second or two. That was enough. The door into the hidden chamber clicked open. He had a brief glimpse of a chamber about three feet wide and six feet deep cut into the rock: he picked up the gun and stepped inside. The door slammed shut.

The blackness was absolute: it made him feel blind. There was no light at all, and no sounds except for faint voices calling out orders or shouting at the women. Then muffled thuds: probably the soldiers banging the walls with their rifle butts as they listened for cavities. Then, faintly, a series of stuttering shots, probably from Schmeissers. Then silence. Now he seemed deaf as well as blind.

He checked that the safety catch was on, and laid the Sten down out of harm's way. He unbuckled his small pack and ammunition pouches and placed them against the wall. The pouches were empty. All the ammunition he had was in the Sten's magazine, and he'd fired a few bursts since reloading. A

133

dozen rounds, perhaps? His Colt revolver he hadn't fired at all. He held it as he groped his way to the door and felt delicately all around the edges, looking for a catch to unlock it. There wasn't one. He gave the door a gentle shove. It was solid. Unless he were let out, he couldn't get out. Perhaps the cell had built as a prison rather than a hideout?

He sat down with his back to the wall. It was stuffy. Was there an air inlet? If there were, perhaps he could smoke. He touched the cigarette packet in his breast pocket. Oh, God, he then realised: Natasha had the matches. They were English. If the Germans found them the women, at the very least, would be taken away for questioning. Would they break and give him away? Not that it mattered one way or the other: if he were left here, he'd die in a few days. Yet they might consider it a kindness to tell the Germans where he was, thinking he'd at least stay alive as a POW, not knowing that captured Commandos were automatically shot. He remembered the crump of the explosive charges and hoped again that the bridge was down.

He thought (why? at a time like this?) of Ugolino. His water bottle was empty. A slow death need not be his, though. He had a revolver. Unless he could gouge his way to lock with his knife? Except the door was a good three feet thick, For a time he slept. The silence was absolute and the blackness was broken only when he put his luminous watch close to this eye to read the time. It told the hours so slowly he took it off his wrist and put in his pocket, looking at it only from time to time. He concentrated on controlling his thoughts and mind. Now and then he stood up to stretch and pace the two or three steps between door and back wall. After twelve hours in the dark he was desperately thirsty and hungry. He hadn't been betrayed, that was clear. But what was going on up there? Out there?

Another three hours passed. And then, without a sound, Natasha opened the door. It was dark outside. She stood in the doorway with the storm lantern, now trimmed so it burned more brightly. "I'm sorry it's been so long," she said. "The Germans had guards here all day. The bridge is down and they're very angry. Tanks, tanks, guns, guns, crossing it, crossing it, day and night. Now it's gone. Could it lose them the War in Italy?"

"It all helps." He gathered up his equipment and followed

her by lamplight. "Did they hurt you?" he asked as they climbed the stairs out of the cellar.

"No. Just shouted a lot. They also fired a lot of bullets into our hay." She pointed over to where it took up a quarter of the barn. "In case you were under it, yes?"

"Probably."

Maria and her daughter waited in the faint starlight outside the barn. "I'm so proud of Carla," Maria said, holding her daughter close.

"She's a good girl," Tomlinson agreed as he stopped in the doorway buckling on his equipment.

"No," Carla cried in distress. "Why are you doing that?"

"I have to go," Tomlinson explained. "You're in danger while I'm here."

"Stay the night," Maria said, "in the ...", not knowing the English word she pointed in the direction of the cell in the barn.

"It'll be safer for all of us if you do," Natasha added. "You won't get far in the dark and you'll need a guide who knows the mountains. In any case, the Partisans will come for you eventually. Soon."

"And we haven't had supper," said Carla. "We waited for you."

"Well," said Tomlinson, "that clinches it." He unbuckled his belt again and followed the two women and the girl into the first Tuscan farm house in which he'd ever set foot. Supper was a bowl of thin vegetable soup with stale bread and hard, salty Parmesan cheese which broke into lumps when you tried to eat it. With it they had a wine which was barely drinkable. "*Proprio brutto vino*," Maria apologised.

"Proper brutal wine?" Tomlinson, who spoke no Italian, suggested by way of translation, guided solely by the sounds.

It felt strangely old-fashioned to eat by lamplight. A small fire and an oil lamp threw shadows on solid rustic furniture. "We have – we had – a house in town," Maria explained. "It's safer here. The farm has been in my mother's family for a hundred years. We stayed here as children. Who knows when it will all end? Not long now?"

Tomlinson, a mere Captain employed to blow up small things such as bridges, didn't know how long either. After supper, feeling guilty at eating their food, he asked: "How can I pay you? How could I ever re-pay you?"

Carla said: "After the war you can buy us ice cream in Lucca. Mamma says it's the best the world."

"Is that true?" Tomlinson asked.

"True that it's the best, or true that I said so?"

"That it's the best."

"Children should always try for the best," Maria said.

"After the war, then," Tomlinson said to Carla. "I'll buy you the best ice cream ever."

"Promise?"

"Promise."

"You have to come back now. You can't break a promise."

For bedding they gave him two blankets, and straw. The straw he refused. He would sleep in the hay: nothing would induce him ever again to go into that cell. But the hay was soft and he slept well, although with his boots on. Next morning Maria came for him very early. He picked up his weapons and equipment and followed her. The hills threw long shadows over the house. She noticed him looking at the stencilled Mussolini, and the slogan, on the wall. "The leader is never wrong," she translated for him with a well practised straight face.

"How old is Carla?" he asked as they crossed the farm yard.

"Eight. Nine very very soon."

He almost said she had two mothers, but thought better of it: mothers being notoriously touchy. But Maria said it for him: "Carla is a lucky girl. She has two mothers."

Breakfast was a bowl of coffee, made from roasted acorns, and *polenta*, made from chestnuts. The *polenta* was so hard you had to cut it with a knife. "Solid porridge?" Tomlinson said, to Carla's loud joy. "I can't go on eating your food," he went on. "You can't have enough for yourselves."

"Can you work?" said Natasha. "Until the Partisans come. There's a lot to do. We have a vegetable patch. We need firewood and water. Lots of things need repairing."

"Yes. Of course. Anything to pay my way."

"Could you help us first to kill Herman," Maria then said. "Now, Carla, we can't feed Herman any more."

"We've fed him for four months," Natasha added. "And

he's very hungry now."

"That's horrible," said the child. "I won't eat him."

"Well, all right, but if we eat him, there'll be more food for you because we won't be hungry. And we can trade him for rice. You like rice."

"Who's Herman?" Tomlinson asked, not unreasonably. "Not what he seems, I hope."

"No," said Maria. "Carla, what is *maiale* in English?"

"Pig." And she left the kitchen.

Maria turned back to Tomlinson. "Can you help?"

He thought it over. "I could shoot him. With the revolver, probably. But what about the noise?"

"Wait for the bombers," said Natasha. "Idiots fire at them all the time. Another shot wouldn't be noticed."

"What about the butchery afterwards? It's a skilled job."

"We've done a bit of that," Natasha told him. Judging by her accent, her family must have had servants in her childhood; almost certainly she'd have had a nanny and a nursery. "War teaches you a lot of things, Captain," she said as though reading his mind.

"What about using a knife?" Tomlinson then added as an afterthought.

"Herman might be too slippery," said Natasha. "After all you're not a slaughter man," she added completely innocent of any irony. Herman was a small but active pig but between them they cornered him in his stye. Tomlinson had put together a kind of silencer out of straw, canvas, and string, thinking all the while that it was more likely to catch fire than stop the noise. They didn't have to wait long: around mid-morning squadrons of Lancasters flew north. As they roared overhead, he pulled the trigger. Afterwards the butchery was messy, but even Carla relented in the end.

Later that day, they found some civilian clothes for him. Whoever the man was, he was shorter than Tomlinson but they let out the cuffs of the sleeves and the turn-ups. His soft, raiding shoes were changed for wooden-soled sandals, and no socks. Nobody had new clothes or even clothes in good repair. If he was caught outside by anybody, the women told him to act as though he were both deaf and dumb. Because he didn't look Italian, they vaguely thought he might pass as Natasha's brother: Natasha, born English, was a naturalised Italian with all the proper papers. Tomlinson went along with it without believing for a moment that it would work.

They worked out all the lines of sight inside of which he couldn't be seen by anybody across the valley. Then he familiarised himself with the places where he was allowed to go. Water came from a spring higher up in the woods. A stream flowed down from it into, and out of, a big stone cistern. A second, shallower, cistern a little farther down the hill was the open-air laundry where clothes and bed linen were cleaned once a week by beating them on a kind of built-in wash-board. Nearby, an out-door oven was where bread had been baked when flour had been plentiful. Now it roasted acorns and chestnuts for coffee and palenta. Anywhere in front of the house was out of bounds to him. That included the pasture lower down the hillside where Bella, their cow, grazed during the day. Natasha was the milkmaid, Carla the cowherd. Every evening she drove Bella up to the barn to be milked.

That night Tomlinson slept on straw in the loft under the tiles (with his wooden soled sandals off). Day by day after that, they settled into a strange kind of domesticity. He discovered he was a natural handyman. That second evening, he found a wheelbarrow with broken spokes in an outhouse. Immediately he set about carving new ones, whittling sticks to length. He even contrived to make an iron tyre from a hoop which had held the staves of a barrel together. The kitchen fire was his forge. He ended up with a wheel-able barrow, its axle greased by a bit of Herman. Next morning, he wheeled manure from the now empty stye to the vegetable patch where they grew potatoes, beans and tomatoes.

That morning, too, Maria set off with bits of Herman in a rucksack and two black bags of a material they called 'American cloth.' The Germans had long since confiscated their bicycles and Maria walked, not to the fortified garrison, but to a smaller town a thousand feet lower and not far above the plain. She was gone all day and came back exhausted in the evening. In the rucksack and bags she now carried Black Market rice and bread (the bread ration, Natasha told him, was only four or five pounds a month), salt (in short supply west of the mountains), a few inches of salami and cheese.

They'd talked about whether he should go armed or not. Tomlinson argued that if he were armed, they could make out he'd forced himself on them and held them by force. Maria argued it would make no difference and in the end she won. Uniform and weapons were locked in the cell in the cellar. If they had warning, Tomlinson could flee into the mountains.

Meanwhile, he settled into a routine. The *gabinetto* – the earth closet – was his job also. He made a new seat, with an uncircular hole, out of a plank. Simple snares he made out of pegs and loops of wire. He set them in the woods and even caught a few rabbits that way, both for the home pot and for trading or giving to the few visitors who came along. Not many: the young men were either, like him, in hiding or still in the Army somewhere (the Garibaldi Division in Russia in fact never came home).

For a few hours a week, he also turned into a schoolmaster teaching Carla what little of the physics, chemistry, biology and arithmetic he remembered from his Sixth Form days, four years ago: he'd been in the Army and at war ever since. He also taught the girl a more colloquial English than she already knew. Literature and history (English) Natasha dealt with. Literature and history (Italian) were left to Maria. Music lessons were suspended for the duration because the piano was so badly out of tune

After Carla had gone to bed, the three adults sat in the big kitchen together. Usually they had a glass of local wine which was pretty awful: *Vine Lavorati* was how Maria described – 'worked over wine'. Some wasn't even made from grapes. One evening, he tasted it, held it up to the lamp light, then tasted it again. "You don't like our wine tonight?" Maria, noticing, asked him.

"It seems a bit different tonight. Better, in fact. Is it?"

"Do you know about wine?" Natasha asked him.

"Nothing whatever."

"Perhaps you have a natural talent, then. It is different."

"After the war," Maria said (they spoke about after the war a lot), "you could sell our wine to people in England. We'd all we very rich again."

"Only if you change the way it tastes."

"My family have a vineyard on the mountains over there." She indicated somewhere south of the city on the hill. "Perhaps we can do better."

"And if ever they have money again in England," Tomlinson added. He sat in silence for a while. "You never talk about Carla's father."

The two women looked at each other. "My husband died before the war," Maria said. Natasha still looked at her, and she nodded.

"My husband was Carla's father," Natasha then explained. "He was an artist."

"Would I now his work?"

"No. But his name was Gideon Comely. We have most of his paintings here."

"Can I see them?"

"They're not expensive," said Maria, meaning (he supposed) not valuable.

Taking the storm lantern with the long wire handle, the three of them climbed into the loft. Natasha said candlelight would be better but they had no candles. The paintings were stacked in a small room at the end of the house farthest away from where he slept. Art had meant little to Tomlinson, the avant garde meant nothing at all, certainly not as the vanguard of things to come. In Gideon's figurative paintings, however, he saw recognisable images. How odd are the ups and downs of war, he thought, as he knelt in the attic of a farm house in Tuscany looking at pigment spread on canvas by a dead English soldier with the painter's widow on one side, his lover on the other. The sheer strangeness of it all was brought home more powerfully by the last picture: a bridge with tall elegant piers, spanning a peaceful valley. The two women looked at him.

"Is that the bridge we demolished?"

"Yes."

"It was beautiful."

They sat in the lamplight in silence for a while. "At the end of the last War," Natasha began again. "Gideon was terribly wounded. Not physically. Mentally. We came to Tuscany in 1923. It was painting which saved him, cured him I suppose you could say."

"I can imagine," said Tomlinson. And then: "Wouldn't the paintings be better in the secret room in the cellar?"

"No," Natasha and Maria said together. "If anything happens to us," Natasha explained, "somebody will find Gideon's work here in time."

For several more weeks all was peaceful. Only once was there a scare. Tomlinson was in the woods checking his snares when, again, Carla came running to him. "*Milizia*," she said when she caught her breath. The Fascist Militia, recently re-formed, wore a uniform of sorts (Tomlinson never saw them) and were armed with carbines and sub-machine guns. "The dregs," was how Maria summed them up.

"How many?"

"Lots. Twelve? Twenty?"

"Will they hurt your mother and Natasha?"

"They don't think so. They told me to tell you to keep hidden."

They heard shouting. "They speak in *dialetto*. In dialect. Natasha doesn't understand it. Mamma does." He told Carla to stay in the woods while he moved down closer to the farm yard. It seemed wrong to skulk in the background but stepping out meant he'd be taken and the Germans would shoot all three. As it was, Maria held her ground, the *milizia* shouted a lot and then left. Even they could see the War wasn't going their way. Besides, when it was all over, Maria's family would probably have influence again.

The end, in fact, came very suddenly. Tomlinson was hoeing in the vegetable garden when Carla called him. She was upset and crying. "Germans?" he asked her. "*Milizia*?"

She shook her head and long dark hair. "Partisans. They've come to take you away."

Tomlinson put his arms around her. "I'll be back, I promise. I promise you." And so finally he put on his uniform and buckled on his equipment again. Half a dozen wild looking men waited for him: they looked like bandits, each with his bandolier. Dangerously, Natasha got out an old Box Brownie to photograph Tomlinson. The *Banda*, wisely, refused.

CHAPTER 21

Harry Tomlinson turned out to be an upright man in (as they'd already worked out) his early eighties: he was slim, strangely not too wrinkled, and – like Carla – he limped. He began by showing them the two pictures which dominated one wall of his living room. Both were bridges. One was the original of the reproduction they'd already seen in Carla's gallery, as well as on the wine bottle labels. It was the one which Tomlinson had helped to demolish in 1944: an elegant bridge rising high above the gorge on delicate arches. Next to it was a stark black and white photograph of the new bridge, un-elegant, clumsy, on concrete piers. Near them on the wall was what looked to Porlock like a regimental badge: a crowned bugle.

Tomlinson, who seemed to favour hard ground with paved paths and stone pots, lived in an old farm house quite high up the valley, in sight both of Carla's orange coloured farmhouse (one of a scatter of farms in what looked like forest) and the bridge. A small stream ran through the grounds, exiting as a short waterfall. Above them in the distance rose the white cliffs of the marble quarries. The old farm house windows had been replaced by a wall of glass. Living room and garden glided into each other. Porlock and Tomlinson spent a good twenty minutes together in the garden

"What will now happen to Mr Maddox and my son?"

"Nothing, I imagine."

"Nothing?"

"Margot owns the painting. She won't want to prosecute."

"No? Why not?"

"Maddox's wife is a close friend. There's a daughter to take into account, as well. A young girl – a child – eight or nine years old."

"What will you do?" the Major asked.

"Nothing."

"Accessory after the fact, Mr Porlock?"

"There's no fact to be an accessory after. No crime has been committed until Margot says there has."

"Mr Maddox goes free?"

"I expect this little escapade has cost him quite a bit, all in all. But, yes, otherwise he probably will go free, along with the unknown Italian man called Gino."

"Not all that unknown, perhaps. I think this Gino works for me."

"In the winery?"

"I have my suspicions and it all fits. Somebody knew of Carla's gallery. It's not publicly or widely known. Narrows it down a bit, don't you think?"

"What will happen to him?"

"I'll probably give him a pay rise," the Major said. "You look shocked."

"That, no doubt, is because I am."

"Gino has the makings of a fine wine master. In any case, it's impossible to fire anybody – anybody on the payroll, that is – in Italy if you employ more than fifteen people. I do."

"Literally impossible to sack anybody?"

"Almost quite literally."

"I see."

"I don't think you do. You can't know just how bad institutionalised corruption is in Italy. Berlusconi did, I think, want to modernise the country. At first, at least. Now, of course, I suppose he'll be remembered for *bunga-bunga* parties. Or as a walking advert for blue pills. Joining the euro was a bad move, too, I think. God know how it'll work out but Germany and Italy are just too different to live together."

"Like the Odd Couple?"

"Oh, worse than that. At least the Odd Couple had a culture and a language in common. No, a disaster is on its way."

"As bad as that?"

"Italy isn't one country, Mr Porlock. Some say it's two – north and south. Personally, I think still the land of the Renaissance city states."

143

"But you've thrived here."

"With a lot of help. The Simonetti family is old. Carla's ancestors were like the Lords of Lucca in the Middle Ages. Times are changing but families are still important here."

"Well," said Porlock (who was finding it unusually easy to talk this old man), "without the rule of law, who else can you trust?"

"Precisely."

"But Gino must have family?"

"It's not Carla's but, yes, he has connections."

"But he tried to cheat Carla."

"Well, I don't know about that. We don't know, at this stage, that he's actually done anything wrong. He knew about Carla's bit of land and he may have been led into wanting to enter into a partnership to develop it. He'd have known about Gideon's gallery. But I don't believe he knew the painting was stolen. He'd know Maddox and my son as successful business men and would have left any deals or dealings with them. He is a very young man."

"So the villain of the piece is Freddie?"

"No, Mr Porlock," Tomlinson said emphatically. "The villain of the piece is my son. He's the axis around which all of this revolves."

"And what will happen to him?"

The Major looked at him. "If Mrs Montague doesn't prefer charges, I don't know. I just don't know. When you pay a public school to educate your child, Mr Porlock, you're buying self-confidence. That's what they sell, that's what you buy. They don't cheat and usually they give you your money's worth. It's undentable. My son has is it in abundance. In spades, as they say. What I can't understand is why he's so attracted to criminality and – more than that – why does he have talk like a Cockney villain in a TV show?"

"A fantasist? Personality Disorder?" Then, afraid he'd gone too far, Porlock reined in.

But the Major wasn't offended. "His mother died soon after he was born. There is that, I suppose. You know about such things, Mr Porlock?"

"No, no, not a lot. Just what I've read. On the internet actually. Narcissistic Personal Disorder comes in at least four varieties – shrinking violets, egoists, collectivists and cynics. The key ingredient is they think they're good, in the sense of being superior, and so can do no wrong."

"I see. I see it's time for me to say 'I see'."

Porlock was more and more relaxed in the old man's company. That knot or balloon of anxiety in the chest unravelled (or deflated). They strolled along the path behind the low garden wall: standing too long put a strain on the Major's gammy leg.

"Your company have been badgering Margot lately," Porlock began again.

"That will stop" said the Major. "Never was part of our sales territory, any way. Mr Maddox will have to look elsewhere for his wine." Then he too changed the subject: "Baby Boomers like my son," he said, "do you think they've had things too easy? "

"Yes."

"Do you understand them?"

"No, but I have read about them."

"Read whom?"

"Scruton, I think. For them, the truth is what their emotions tell them it is. If their feelings change, the truth changes as well. Their connection with history is broken, too, so they can't learn from the past. On top of all this, the Cultural Marxists got at them. They've been inoculated with that particular mindset and can't break free of it. In fact, they don't seem to know that it is a mindset at all – just another piece of received, second-hand software. They think it's a universal truth which they've thought out for themselves. Too much self-esteem, too little reason for it. It's like a collectivised Personality Disorder."

"Sounds a bit like Tony Blair?"

"Exactly. The archetypical Boomer."

"We sound like a couple of old fogeys, Mr Porlock. Are we?"

"Yes, Major, I suspect we are."

They stood silently for a while in the warm evening air. The Major pointed to the bridge with his stick. "The elegant old. The monstrous new. Our intelligence was faulty. The usual snafu. A German infantry battalion, which we didn't know about, was standing by in the town. We got the bridge. They got us. I was the only survivor. Thanks to Carla's two mums. Thanks to Carla, too."

"Not wounded?"

"The leg came later. On another bridge. Over an oily canal in Holland. Heroics are over-rated."

"Do you really believe that?"

"No, but it's not the done thing to say so, not any more."

"I really do believe that heroism is one of the heights of human achievement," Porlock said, revealing his inner thoughts in a way he'd never done before. "Not for me, though. I've never been in a war but if had I wouldn't have fared well. The heroic is beyond my range. For me, the body has always been just a machine for carrying the mind. So it's easy for me to say that war might have its merits in creating a space where high heroism can happen. In the abstract, at least, heroism expands us. Growth, as I see it, is what life's all about. War's deplorable thought war is, I suppose. Being a child in the Second World War probably gives me a false perspective."

"Well, yes, it's fashionable to deplore war, isn't it? And of course it is deplorable and horrible. At the same time, though, you're right. For a young man it can be a very great adventure. I've never been freer than when I was in uniform." He pointed across the valley with his stick, tracing an invisible path along the hillside. "Early one morning I followed Carla along a footpath over there, all around the contour of the hills. The Germans were looking for me. In strength. They shot Commandos out of hand, you know. No POW Red Cross parcels for us, or reading for degrees in accountancy. But what an extraordinary thing to happen to a young man. Hiding in an hidden chamber, then setting up some kind of family life with the finest people I'd ever met, and all in a foreign country. I'd never been abroad before. I was a fairly junior clerk with the Great Western Railway in Truro."

"I can imagine," said Porlock. "With envy, if I'm to be honest."

"Most men – at least the best men – would say the same. And yet, or course, a lot of men died here that night," he went on, looking up at the bridge. "That's the horrible part. The really horrible part. You become so close to your comrades in arms – forgive the old fashioned language – and to have them all killed in the space of an hour leaves a gap you can never fill. All the same, it's an extraordinary thing for a young man to be involved in. Young men need extraordinary things, I suppose. It seems to be wired into them. Some of them at least. Most of them."

"Did you go far, with the Partisans?"

"No, as it happened, not far at all. The DCLI had just about taken the monastery – a fortress, really – at Incontro. We went there."

"DCLI? Duke of Cornwall's Light Infantry? Is that why you have their badge on your wall? Next to Gideon's painting of the old bridge?"

"And the photograph of the hideous new? Partly. It was Gideon's old mob, as well. In the Great War, of course. I felt quite small when I got to Incontro. I'd just helped blow up a bridge. Those boys specialised in rivers and mountains. crossing and climbing them under fire."

"Amalgamated out of business now, of course."

"Well, yes, but amalgamated into business in the first place. The South Devons, I think, and a Cornish regiment without a Duke in sight."

"Do you ever feel we're living at the end of our history?"

"It's not our world, is it?" Mr Tomlinson asked.

"It never has been mine," Porlock replied truthfully.

"After the War I went into the wine trade. Not Tuscan at first because until the 1970s Italian wine was virtually unexportable. Unimportable, at least. But I came here as often as I could and set up the winery when it became possible to do so. Carla's family is influential in these parts, as I've just said. I think I'd have been driven out otherwise. As would have happened to Mr Maddox and my son, once the locals had fleeced them."

Carla and Kate had been talking together all this while in the living room. Gina, the housekeeper, was cook. Now the two old men were called in to eat.

"I used to have a pet name for Carla when she was a little girl," Tomlinson said as he limped towards the open window/wall into his house. "Carling. Carla plus darling. She thought it very witty and clever. Then we heard it's the name of a lager. You can't call a well-bred Italian lady from the Chianti wine country by the name of a Danish beer, can you?"

"Hardly."

Porlock's habitual nervousness came back in the dining room – although he was getting better, with relapses: one pace forward, but only half a pace back these days. When they were all seated, he asked Carla how much she knew about her father's pre-Italian history. Tomlinson took it on himself to answer. "Well, let's see," he began. "Name Gideon Groundlees Comely. Born 1894. Quite a wealthy family. Made their money in Jute, I think. Public school. Then, in 1912, Oxford. That means he graduated, I assume, in 1915. Probably went straight into the Army. Duke of Cornwall's Light Infantry. Rank of captain at Passiondale, the 3rd Battle of Ypres. Soon after that, he turned up at Craiglockhart, the hospital for shell-shocked officers near Edinburgh. Post-traumatic stress disorder I think it's called nowadays. The posh word then was neurasthenia. Possibly took up painting in the hospital, as a kind of therapy. And then early in the 1920s he came here to Tuscany. Stayed for the rest of his life. I don't think he ever set foot England again. And he missed the last War, of course. Died of an infected minor wound in 1939. Very attractive to women, too, I should add."

"Harry!" Carla said.

"There's nothing 'Harry!' about it," the Major persisted.

"He lived with two of the finest, and Carla knows it. One was her mother. The other was Gideon's wife. Do you know how brave they were during the war?"

"No," Kate said. Porlock shook his head, his mouth being full.

"The Fascists had an armed political militia called the Black Shirts. The equivalent of the SS was called OVRA. OVRA were also a bit like the East German Stasi. Fascist spies spied on other Fascist spies and both spied on non-Fascists. Nobody knew who to trust. Which was one point of the exercise of course. You couldn't plot against Mussolini because you couldn't trust anybody. They took a terrible risk with Carla as well. She was just about old enough to join the *Piccole Italiane*. That was a kind of militarised Brownie pack but without a muddle-headed Joyce Grenfell as Brown Owl. Somehow they kept Carla hidden over there. The day she found, me she'd broken away to find out what the explosions had been all about. And then of course they risked

risked their lives to shelter me. Not many of us can attract good women like that."

"No," Porlock agreed. Kate looked at him sharply.

"Harry," Carla said, "you mustn't talk like that. We're three and a half old-fashioned English people: immodesty isn't cricket, is it, Joshua?"

"On this occasion it is," he replied. "If that's all right?"

"Kate?"

"I'm with Joss."

"Carry on then, Major," Carla laughed.

The talk returned, naturally, to the War and its aftermath. "I sometimes wonder," Tomlinson said, "if the War didn't make the Welfare State in England inevitable. People got used to having every decision made for them. The average soldier in barracks was told what to wear each morning – best BD, shirt sleeve order, fatigues or whatever. It was infantilising. Civilians too were ordered about. Bevin Boys. Reserved occupations. Rationing. People came to rely on bureaucrats."

"What about the Education Corps?" Porlock said. "I've read something about their radicalising the troops?"

"The Marxist sergeants in the RAEC? Yes, I heard about them at them the time. They were particularly busy in Egypt when the War moved into mainland Europe. A lot of troops were surplus to requirements and got left behind. I suppose there wasn't a lot for them to do and a good few of them never got used to working ever again, back in Civvie Street, that is, when they'd been demobbed."

"Orwell had a lot to say about their civilian counterparts," Porlock went on. "But even then they weren't original. They were the heirs of late Victorians like William Morris and E M Forster."

"I think the Major is a bit of a pessimist, Joshua," Carla said. "Are you?"

Kate looked across the table at Porlock. 'Go on', her look said.

"About the future of the West, yes, I suppose I am. It's probably temperamental," he added, backtracking as usual, "rather than rational. But then again what do I know?"

"There's always been roguery," said Carla.

Again Kate willed Porlock on. "Well, yes," he said, "but there was always greatness as well. It's as though the spectrum has been shortened – instead of running from bad to very great, it now goes from very bad to not-all-that-good. Greatness is today's missing ingredient."

"What do you mean by greatness," Kate asked, although she thought she knew the answer.

"Great minds, great pride, great confidence, great art, great poetry, great ideas. The West seems to have flattened out into a continuum where everybody conforms to the same ways of thinking. Science is being corrupted too. Surely that's something new and very ominous?"

"It wasn't just the movies that got smaller?" Carla said.

"No, the Gloria Swansons have shrunk as well."

"What's the cause, do you think?" the Major asked.

"The loss of a sense of something greater than themselves."

"So we're back to *Gideon's God*?" Carla said.

"Well, that's just personal to me." He came to a halt again, then limped on: "By something greater I don't necessarily mean God. It could be patriotism, for example. But, as I say, what do I know?'

"Well, you must know if you'd like coffee or not?"

"Oh, coffee, please," said Porlock, fretful because he thought he'd give too much of himself away, and made a fool of himself as well.

Coffee, at first, promised to be to a peaceful end to a strange day. But after it was served, the strangest thing of all unfolded

Carla brought out an album of photographs dating back to the 1920s and '30s, including the one Natasha had unwisely taken of Harry Tomlinson in the War. (The bottom quarter was fogged: the upper part showed a tall, lean, smiling young man in the uniform of the 1940s British Army.)

One whole page was filled with a large photograph of Gideon Comely. He was a handsome man (he lived up to his name) of around forty with a half smile and the serenity which some people achieve after great turmoil. But that wasn't the thing which startled Kate so much. She and Porlock were sitting together on a settee. She turned the album for him to see the picture of Gideon. "Do you have the first memory chip for the camera in your belt?"

He had. He took the current chip out of the camera and slotted in the old one. He switched on the camera and clicked through the first photographs he'd taken. He found the one he was looking for, zoomed in, reframed it, and passed the camera to Kate.

"What is it?" said Carla. "You both look as though you've seen a ghost."

"I knew there was something about you," Kate said, "something that's half-bothered me off and on all day. At first I thought we must have met somewhere, but that isn't it. We never have. Now I see it." She handed the camera over and the album. "That's Margot," she explained. "You and her have very similar features, particularly the eyes and the nose. Looking at the photographs of Mr Comely, I just wonder if that's where they come from."

For a full minute Carla said nothing, looking from one picture to the other. Then: "Do I have a sister?"

"Margot doesn't know who her father was," Porlock explained. "She once told us she is eighty-one which means she was conceived in the summer of 1923. Gideon was certainly there at the time – that's the date on the *Gideon's God* painting."

"It seems I do have a sister." Carla passed the camera and album over to Major Tomlinson.

"DNA's a surer way," said Tomlinson. "But the resemblance is pretty conclusive, I'd say. The age difference is the only problem. The daughter is twice as old as the father in these pictures."

"Joss?" Kate said.

"Ah, yes, hang on a minute," Porlock said. "I may be able to help there as well." He took the camera back from the Major and worked back through all the earliest pictures he'd taken. "Is there a photograph of Carla's father as a young man in the album?" he asked as he found shot he was looking for – the painting of Margot as a young woman. He handed the camera to Carla along with the album.

Carla spent two or three minutes this time looking from one image to the other. "Joss, Kate," she said at last. "Do you have my sister's number in your phones."

Later that night, driving back to their hotel, Porlock said: "I don't think I can take much more. All we need now is for *Gideon's God* to turn in extraordinary circumstances."

Flashforward: early next morning

Freddie was cautious enough to use a land line. "Gabriel? Things have hit the fan. Somebody's put the frighteners on Gino."

"Who has?"

"Search me. I can guess. This is Italy. The Mafia, I suppose."

"But Gino's well-connected."

"Not well enough, it seems. This country's corrupt from top to bottom."

"What's gone wrong?"

"Gino's only gone and dumped the daub on the old trout's doorstep, hasn't he? Free and for gratis. He's been playing up something chronic for some time now. I had to speak sharply to him in the winery to give him a bit of backbone."

"Why didn't he just burn it?"

"Search me. Italians are supposed to like art or something, aren't they?"

"Could be. Still, we've lost one of our bargaining chips?"

"You could put it that way."

"Never a crucial one. Does the old girl know about you? And Anson's, I mean?"

"Give me some credit. Gabriel. I'm not completely wet behind the ears."

"I know, Freddie, I know that. The provenance old Bradshaw cooked up should keep us out of the frame. The old girl can't trace it back to the old boiler on that island. You know what, Freddie? Those old women are going to be the death of me."

"Tell me about it."

"We've lost a game, Freddie, not a set and certainly not the match. It's not the end of the earth. We live to play another day. We're covered from all angles and nobody's on our tail."

Later that morning

Porlock took the call at six thirty next morning from a very excited Carla. "Joss? Have I woken you?"

"No. No, not at all."

"*Gideon's God* is here."

"I beg your pardon?"

"Somebody left it on my doorstep during the night."

"Who left it?"

"We don't know, although Harry thinks he does."

"Gino?"

"Harry thinks so. Can you come back?"

"Of course. What time?"

"Any time you like. We're all up. Have breakfast with us."

"We're on our way. Have you told Margot?"

"I'm just about to."

"Is it beautiful? The painting?"

"See for yourself."

"You sound excited."

"I am."

"Does that mean it's good?"

"The sooner you stop asking questions, the sooner you'll see for yourself."

"I'll rouse Kate."

It was another beautiful day – cool in the bright morning sunshine which coloured the painted house fronts but kept the marble crags in the shade. Porlock carried the usual balloon of anxiety and elation in his chest – lifted by his success, dampened by fear of let-down. Pre-breakfast breakfast was a couple of packets of biscuits, eaten in the car.

"Can't you go any faster?" he asked with his mouth full.

"No."

"Exciting, isn't it?"

"Yes."

"Then why can't we go faster?"

"An extra ten minutes won't make any difference. Don't be so impatient, Joss."

"I'm not impatient."

"You are. Have another biscuit."

"Carla will be giving us breakfast."

"It'll be lunch if you stand gawping at the picture too long," Kate said, slowing down to let a lorry overtake.

"Somebody should make a movie about this."

"Who'd play you? Hugh Grant?"

"Who's he?"

"'Goodness, Joss, you are an old fogey. You know who Gloria Swanson was, but not who Hugh Grant is."

"Both old *and* a fogey? Whatever happened to mature?"

"Some times you're very mature," Kate admitted. "At other times you're like a little boy."

"I'm sorry about that."

"I'm not. You're my little boy. I wouldn't have you any other way."

"Oh?"

"Yes, 'Oh?'. Which street do we want?"

"Keep going. God, I hope the painting's good. What will do if it's rotten?"

"See what I mean? Little boy."

"Turn left here."

"You're good at remembering directions."

"Oh? Good at nothing else?"

"I don't want you getting big headed."

"I feel I've achieved something here. Set out to do

something and done it. Don't I get credit for that?"

"Just a bit."

"Gosh, though, I do hope the painting's good enough to be worth it."

"What you've done is worthwhile on its own. Margot and Carla will always be grateful."

"If they get on when they meet next week."

"They will."

"How you know that?"

"I know them both and I know they will."

"Kate, have you always been self-assured and bossy?"

"Yes."

"And it's never bothered you?"

"No. Is this the turning?"

"Yes, it is. The Moment of Truth, eh?"

Kate stopped the car and pulled up the hand brake. She looked at Porlock: "Ready?"

"Yep."

"Come on then."

Carla had set the draped canvas on an easel facing the padded bench in her private gallery. She was going to unveil the painting as if it were special event, a special occasion – which for Porlock, of course, it was: he'd come a long way and overcome a lot of obstacles to be here in the suffused light of a gallery in a private house in Tuscany.

"Ready?"

Porlock nodded. Carla pulled on the cloth. It slipped off. And there was *Gideon's God 1923*. It was an abstract: different shades of yellow – corn, gold, golden, lemon, saffron, edging into tangerine and amber down through ochre to umber – pouring out of a central point. That was the first impression. The second was of movement as the eye was pulled back down into the yellow middle, like a vortex. You felt you were falling into the centre of things. After several silent minutes Porlock said: "He did it. He painted God. Or so it seems to me."

"Would you like tea or coffee?" Carla asked in her most civilised manner. "In the kitchen? You look shocked."

"Stunned, to be more accurate. "Do we know anything at all about the painting?" Porlock asked.

"No," Carla answered. "Nothing whatsoever."

"No mention in letters? Nothing by word of mouth?"

"No. Natasha never mentioned it. Not that she spoke about their life in England very much, so that's not so surprising."

"Painted, put away, and forgotten for nearly eighty years?"

"While the world changed all around it," Carla added.

"It's an extraordinary story because it's such an extraordinary painting."

"Dashed off, most probably," Carla said.

"Dashed off, may be, but it works."

"You really are impressed, Mr Porlock."

"Yes, I am. I most certainly am. And it bothers me a bit – well, a lot – that we'll probably never know anything about it. Why was it painted? What prompted it? What was in the painter's mind? Where was it painted? Was it in summer? Morning or evening?"

"Do those things matter?" Carla asked. "Does a work of art need a context? Some people would say it doesn't matter."

"It matters to me." One advantage of being an outsider, he thought without speaking, is that you're not constrained to conform to the current fashionable mindset of the educated masses.

"Why don't you stay here for a while on your own. Kate and I will be making coffee in the kitchen. Come through when you're ready."

When they left the gallery, Porlock stood up to get closer to the canvas. He touched it (after wiping a finger dry on his shirt): the paint was almost impasto. He leaned closer until his eyes lost focus. The painting had all the hallmarks of spontaneity – done in a single burst of energy and insight. He took out his camera and photographed it in close up, in bigger close up, in mid shot, in long shot. Then he went into the kitchen and was given a cup of black coffee.

"Well, Joss," Carla said when he'd drunk half of it, "Kate told me yesterday that you and my father are kindred spirits. What have you to say? Please stand up and tell us."

He looked at her, surprised and puzzled. "I'd feel like a lecturer."

"Then begin the lecture, *professore*."

Kate was clearly not being helpful, sitting there looking at him expectantly. "Well, all right." For a moment or two he said nothing as he composed his thoughts. He began: "All the paintings here, I suspect, have the same underlying theme, even the one that seems to be the odd man out, by which I mean the dark brown seascape. I don't think it is the sea. I think it's his last battlefield in the Great War before the poppies grew. If it is the sea, it's the sea turned into corruption right down to its bed. It's what happens when the light goes out."

Neither of the women said anything. He ploughed on. "All the other paintings are about cleansing, in one way or another. They are also about what is unchanging and timeless. They are about things old enough to have been cleansed by time. Many are of sunlight. From a human point of view, sunlight is eternal. You can't pollute sunlight. Air, yes. Sunlight, no. Nor time."

Neither of the women spoke. "I also think there was a door in Gideon's mind which opened on to a different universe. He was only at ease when he went through it. Painting these things was the key to turn the lock. It was as though there was an inner place, then another door leading to a deeper Elsewhere, a Somewhere Else. In that inner-inner place was where he saw … well, the thing I've come all this way to see. And do see."

CHAPTER 23

Kate's taxi drove past the Goldsmiths' bungalow and stopped next door. The sky had clouded over from the west. As he paid the taxi driver, Kate walked between the untrimmed bushes in the front garden and unlocked the front door. By the time he got there, she was deep inside the house with its large 1950s rooms. A corridor passed between two bedrooms and a bathroom. "Where are you?" he called.

"Here."

"Here?"

"In the kitchen."

"Which is where?" He was now in the large living room. To the left was the en suite master bedroom. The kitchen was to the right. Kate came to the door. "In here," she said.

"Big, isn't it?" said Porlock, following her in. All the windows overlooked a big overgrown garden.

"Wonderful. This kitchen needs a lot of work, though. It will have to be rebuilt, really."

"Like Carla's?"

"Like mine. This breakfast area's in the wrong place, to begin with."

"What's that out there?" Porlock asked, nodding towards a long building which ran along the edge of the garden at right angles to the kitchen.

"A utility room, and a work shop," Kate replied. "You can get there through the garage, as well."

"A workshop?"

"With a wash basin. Come upstairs. It's not really a bungalow at all. The last owner converted the loft into a couple of extra rooms." She led the way into the living room where wooden stairs had been built against the inside wall. The floor area of the loft-rooms was big, but the space itself was made smaller by the slope of the roof. Dormer windows had been set into it on either side, one overlooking the front garden, the other the back.

"Can you afford all this, Kate?"

"Not on my own, no. But if we pool what we have, we can."

"You're taking an awful lot for granted."

She took more. "The workshop in the garden can be your studio and you can have the upstairs rooms for a library. We might need a stair lift when you're older. They are a bit steep."

"You're expecting me to settle for domesticity and a dormer window with a glimpse of the sea. *If* I stand on tip-toe?"

"If we lowered the window to floor level, you could see into the garden from your arm chair."

"Kate?"

"This room can wait," Kate went on relentlessly. "We need to get the kitchen done first. I always think a home revolves around the kitchen."

"Kate?" But Kate had gone downstairs. He looked out of the dormer window at the front of the house, feeling the strange silence of an empty room weighing in his ears. It began to rain: he could hear the big new drops pattering on the leaves outside the window pane. Rain, like birdsong, was a key to his kingdom. This unreal solid world shimmered and shifted on the surface of the real unsolid one deep below it. The peace which passeth understanding.

As often happened now, his mind went back to Gideon Comely – what had been in his mind when he painted that picture? Where? When? It depressed Porlock that he'd never know.

"The master bedroom will be beautiful when it's decorated," he heard Kate call up to him. "We'll need a very big double bed. You could hang your copy of *Gideon's God* either there or in the living room. Living room, I think."

Prequel: 21st June 1923

A char-a-banc parks in the new open air bus station which already smells strongly of oil. Passengers disembark for a day by the river or the sea. Among them is Bill Lulworth in a flat cap and a shiny suit, smoking a pipe. He's an upright man who walks quietly along Fore Street, hands behind his back, behind his fretful wife and happy daughter. They're going to take the foot ferry to the swatch of yellow beach over the river. His wife and daughter will cross first, allowing him time to have a pint of beer in the Ferry Inn. The landlord, a short squat man, fills a pint pot for him. It's all beer to the brim with little froth. A regimental badge, the crowned bugle of the Duke of Cornwall's Light Infantry, hangs on the wall behind the bar. The landlord walks with a limp and breathes badly.

"Gas, was it?"

"Shrapnel."

Bill's daughter Dorothy, seven years old and smart in ankle boots and calico smock, pokes her head around the door of the four ale bar. "Dad, can I have some beer?"

"Ask you Mother, pet."

"She'll say no."

"Then no's the answer, petal."

"When I'm big I'll smoke a pipe."

"Girls can't smoke pipes. Ask your Mam. She'll know why."

"When I'm big Mam can't stop me."

"Your Mam's a holy terror, petal. You know that. She rules the roost."

"She don't do what Gran says."

"What?"

"I'm Mam's daughter. Mam is Gran's daughter but Mam don't do what Gran tells her to do."

"All right then," said Bill, laughing. "One sup, but no more, mind."

"Ugh, it's horrid."

"It's meant to be, to stop little girls from drinking it. Ask your Mam." And in his mind he wanders back, as he does so many times a day, to that tot of rum that morning by the river when the barrage lifted, before the whistles blew.

"Penny, Dad?"

"I'm thinking what a clever girl I've got." And he looks through the window at the ferry rowing back over the glinting river and sees young men drowning in shell-made slurry. God rest them all. So much fear, he'd never be afraid again. Mam, clucking, red-nosed and fretful, comes in to shoo her daughter out.

"One pint only, Bill Lulworth. I've made sandwiches out of a whole loaf of bread. I'm not having you wasting them. Do you hear me?"

"I hear you," he says. Shells go crump, crump, crump in his mind.

******

The Olde Copper Kettle is new, opened by two maiden ladies to catch the tripper trade and folk from the char-a-bancs which double-declutch down the hill. Cakes are served on cut-glass three-tiered, paper- doilied, stands. Doilies are cut like lace and lace half-curtains on copper poles cover half the tall windows. Hovis is advertised and Wall's ice-cream. Table knives have mother of pearl handles faintly iridescent in the brightness of the sun.

Two widows in second hand frocks with lopsided hems sit together in a corner, cowed by the gentility of the tea room. They look old and worn out, though probably both have just turned thirty.

"Nice cup of tea, Phyl."

"Very nice, Doll."

"Have my strawberry jam?"

"The pips get under my teeth, love."

"Mine too. Shall we ask for something else?"

"No, don't let's spoil things. It's such a treat to be waited on."

"We won't want our teas."

"Oh, I will, Doll. Make the most of it while it lasts is what I always say."

161

******

It's been a hot day: air seemed to thicken in the heat. In gullies in the hills along the Bramble River, sorrel and hay-scented buckle fern grow by waterfalls, wild garlic among oaks and limes. Shadows now begin to point east. In the ball room of the Rumblestone Inn, a revolutionary and his girl sit on gilded chairs by windows opening on to the terrace and the sea. A quintet in evening gowns play dance tunes among the potted palms in the stern cabin.

"When we achieve power," boasts George Bradshaw, "places like this will be the first to go."

"Oh, for goodness sake, George, it's only a dance."

"Deca-dance, more like."

"It's a bit of fun for holiday makers, not a sin."

"Capitalism's a sin, but we'll bring it down."

"And then what? Tell me that, Georgie Bradshaw. What then?"

"Why, a workers' paradise of course. Four hours work in the morning, Plato in the afternoon."

"And how are you going to get rid of them all? Arsenic in their caviar?"

"Liquidate most of them, set the rest to work."

"They do work, I expect, else how can they live?"

"Off the sweat of the workers' brow, that's how."

A young man sidles up in a haze of bay rum and bath salts. He wears white flannel trousers and a blazer broadly striped in purple, red, and mauve.

"What ho," he addresses the girl. "Care to trip the Antic Hay?"

"Gladly." She flounces on to the polished floor, flounces that is as much as a girl in a tight tube-like frock could flounce. "Do you work?" she asks the young man.

"My word, no, I do assure you I do not."

"He'll kill you then," she said nodding back to where George sat conspicuously on a gilded chair.

"Not the cove in the cloth cap?"

"He's a Revolutionary Socialist."

"Golly! Good of you to let me know."

"Are you staying here?"

"I have a room with a view of the rising sun," he replied.

"Not that I've actually ever seen it."

"Is it handy?"

"Rather. If the dawn does come up like thunder it does so very discreetly."

"No, I meant handy for visiting?"

"Oh, rather. Room fifty-three."

"I'm sick of that bloody revolution."

"I should think so, too. It would give Pa the pip if your pal spreads the last of the Kettlethorpes over the smiling acres."

"How many smiling acres?"

"They cover hill and dale."

"I'm Kitty, by the way."

"Reggie. Enchanted to meet you."

A flash and a loud pop catches them unawares as they complete a graceful swirl. "What was that?" Kitty asks, alarmed.

"Ghastly snapper. Look, the ghastly fellow has changed his bulb and is going for the band." The bulb flashed again and the photographer walked away. "That's the last we'll see of him, thank goodness," says Reggie.

******

Now, in the long summer twilight a young man sets up an easel on the western edge of the island. A young woman joins him. "Why don't we go to the Solstice Ball?" she asks him.

"Paint's the perfect noise for paint, isn't it?" says the young man almost as though he hasn't heard her. He loads his brush with paint and stares at the colour. "Paint sounds like paint, doesn't it? Just as colour sounds like colour. Slide sounds like slide."

"Gideon?"

"Fool is perfect, too," says the young man. "Fool – you blow it out and it pushes people away."

"You're pushing me away. What does that say about you?"

"A brushful of the brightest yellow paint to start with, I think."

"Come on, Gideon, let's join the others at the dance."

163

"Provence?" says Gideon. "No. Not Provence. Tuscany, rather. Florence and Chianti. I'd like that. I'd like to paint olive groves."

"We have orchards here," Natasha says. Then adds: "But, yes, of course you're right. Tuscany is much, much better. Over there, we can start all over again."

"Isolate is a truly terrible word, don't you think? Like desolate."

"You have such a gift, Gideon, but you're throwing it all away. Look at your last painting – a brown sea with brown waves and a red sky. It's so .... unhealthy. And wrong."

"It's called *The Western Front*. That's what it was like. In this one I'm painting a light that's brighter than the sun." He looks at her mildly. "That light is love. And you know what love is, don't you?"

"Yes, Gideon, I think I do."

"Yes, you're right of course. It's God."

"Is now a good time for that kind of thing? Can't we just do simple, ordinary things for a little while? It would do you so much good to dance and laugh with other people. For a little while. Only a little while. Come on now. Be a dear. Let's go to the Ball. I've got your clothes all ready." When he doesn't answer, she says: "You came through the War without a scratch and still you're wounded. Graves was left for dead but *he's* all right."

"Graves? War graves?"

"You could be all right if you want to. You just have to want to. It's all in your mind."

"We'll go to Tuscany and paint olive groves. So much better than graves. What a difference a vowel makes. I think I'll give *this* painting to Margot. As a keepsake."

"We have to get away from that woman, too," says Natasha with some irritation. "She's not for you. She can't go on taking young men to bed to cure them of what happened in the Trenches."

"She has a good heart."

"A good body too," says Natasha tartly, "judging by the effect she has on men."

164

"That also," agrees Gideon quietly. "A woman's body can be a great comfort to men who've been harmed."

"I'm a woman."

"And don't we make love?"

"Physical love shouldn't be about comfort."

For the first time Gideon is checked: he stops painting and presses the brush into the canvas. He was facing south, sideways to the sun but now turns to look at Natasha. "No, you're right of course. It isn't just about comfort. It isn't about comfort at all. There's a terrible deep mystery about love. Can't you see I'm trying to capture it in paint but I can't understand it? I wish I could. If I could understand it, everything would be all right."

Natasha, close to tears, walks to the edge of the island where she stands with her arms folded looking at the sun going down. Gideon starts painting again. Natasha picks up pebbles and throws them down the sharp rocks into the sea. The sea breathes against the rocks, rather than rises or breaks. Even the sun path on the sea is still.

"You're right about Tuscany, as well," Gideon calls to her at last. "Quite right. We'll begin again. We'll go to Tuscany. But first we'll burn the past. Burn the paintings. A great bonfire on the isthmus. At midnight tonight. A pagan pyre on Mid-Summer's Eve. The longest day. The tides meet around midnight tonight. We can wade back through the sea."

"Oh, that would be divine," says Natasha happily. "So romantic. Will there be a moon?"

"It's a clear sky." He goes on painting with quick unthought-out strokes. "I'll keep *The Western Front*. We'll take it to Tuscany with us."

"Wouldn't it be better to forget all that, put all that behind us, when we go away?"

"Say goodbye to it all? No. No. We must never forget the Western Front. We will start again but the Trenches can never be filled in." He mixes the last of the paint. "I don't understand it, but something with a terrible meaning happened over there. Something to do with God, I think. Something ultimate. There," he ends. "It's finished. I've painted God. I believe I've got the likeness right. *God in Paint, 1923*. That's the title."

"Oh, it's beautiful, Gideon. Simply beautiful. Divine."

"Of course it is. It's God."

"You really mean that, don't you? Mean it quite literally?"

"Of course. This and the painting of *The Western Front* go together. Two sides of the same thing. In some way. I don't know how. Or what. Not of this world though. Approaching the ultimate in some way. I wish I understood it. It's something of cosmic import, I do know that. Something to do with God and the Devil. But which is which I just don't know. If I could understand, everything would be all right," he adds, suddenly fretful again.

"Ssh. Ssh. Ssh," Natasha soothes him. "Everything's going to be all right." Then, going back to a kind of normality: "We should keep the two paintings together then."

"Oh, no. No. *God in Paint* is for Margot. They should be separated by space and time."

"Perhaps we can re-unite them in the future?"

"Only after a very long time. Not for a very long time. If ever. It's the great divide, you know."

They stand looking at the painted canvas on the easel for some time. It's a calm evening after a hot day. The sea is smooth to the horizon and around the edges of the blue cliffs. Natasha notices the spot where the brush was pressed down. "Should you paint out the blemish?" she asks.

"No, I don't think so. It was a moment of truth. That spot is the little lost human in the mystery of it all."

"It's still a very beautiful painting," Natasha says again, "but the title's wrong. It's too cold and impersonal. After all, the vision is yours. What about calling it *Gideon's Vision*?"

"Well, yes, but it isn't a vision, is it? It's a portrait."

"*Gideon's God*, then."

"Of course, Natasha. Of course that's the title. *Gideon's God 1923*."

"Do we need the date?"

"Of course. That's what God looks like now. What will He look like in 1943? 1983? 2003?"